SYMPOSIUM

PLATO

SYMPOSIUM

THE BENJAMIN JOWETT TRANSLATION

SUBSTANTIALLY REVISED
BY HAYDEN PELLICCIA

THE MODERN LIBRARY

NEW YORK

1996 Modern Library Edition

Biographical note copyright © 1996 by Random House, Inc.
Introduction and translation revisions copyright © 1996
by Hayden Pelliccia

Jacket painting: detail of Plato from *The School of Athens* by Raphael,
courtesy of Scala/Art Resource, N.Y.

Printed on recycled, acid-free paper.

Library of Congress Cataloging-in-Publication Data is available

ISBN 0-679-60197-X

Manufactured in the United States of America

2 4 6 8 9 7 5 3 1

PLATO

■ ■ ■

Plato was born around 427 B.C. He came from an aristocratic family that had long played a prominent role in Athenian politics. His father claimed descent from Codrus, the last king of Athens, and his mother from Dropides, a kinsman of Solon, the famous Athenian legislator. Although little is known with certainty about the details of Plato's early life, it is generally assumed that he received an education in keeping with a man of noble birth, including a study of the ancient Greek poets. His youth was overshadowed by the great Peloponnesian War that engulfed the peninsula from 431 to 404 B.C., and he may have participated in military engagements during the last years of the conflict. In its aftermath Athens was ruled for a time by an oligarchy of tyrants before democracy was restored. Rejecting a political career, Plato became a follower of the brilliantly unorthodox Socrates around 408 B.C.

The execution of Socrates in 399 B.C. on charges of impiety and corrupting the minds of the young deeply shocked Plato, and he temporarily withdrew from Athens for several years to the neighboring city of Megara. Inspired by Socrates's inquiries into the nature of ethical standards, he sought a cure for the ills of society not in politics but in philosophy. Over the next decade he began writing the philosophical dramas known as Socratic dialogues as a means of commemorating and defending his teacher and friend. Several, probably completed during this period—*Apology, Crito, Euthyphro,* and *Phaedo*—present accounts of the trial and condemnation of Socrates. His other early dialogues include *Ion, Hippias, Protagoras, Laches, Lysis,* and *Gorgias.* In 389 B.C., at roughly the age of forty, Plato journeyed to Italy and Sicily, where he was strongly influenced by Pythagorean thinkers. At this time he also formed a deep affection for his pupil Dion, brother-in-law of the tyrant Dionysius I.

Plato returned to Athens in 387 B.C. and founded the Academy in a sacred park on the outskirts of the city. The first permanent institution devoted to philosophical and mathematical research as well as teaching, it became the model for all modern Western universities. The school prepared young men for public life by emphasizing science rather than rhetoric as the source of all wise political action. It is believed that the *Republic,* Plato's central work offering a vision of the ideal state, dates from the interval between 386 and 367 B.C. when he lectured at the Academy. Also attributed to this prolific period in Plato's career are a number of celebrated dialogues: *Menexenus, Euthydemus, Meno, Cratylus, Symposium, Phaedrus, Parmenides,* and *Theaetetus.*

At the request of Dion, Plato traveled to Sicily in 367 B.C. in order to test his ideas about the education of a philosopher-king on an actual reigning statesman, Dionysius II, the new ruler of Syracuse. Plato tried to instruct the young Dionysius in the curriculum of the Academy, but the scheme failed. According to some accounts Plato barely escaped alive, and the tyrant actually held the philosopher prisoner when he again visited Syracuse in 361 B.C. to repeat the experiment. In 366 B.C. Aristotle enrolled in the Academy and remained there over the last twenty years of Plato's life. So remarkable a pupil was Aristotle that Plato referred to him as "the mind of the school." During this time the philosopher probably composed his final dialogues: *Politicus, Timaeus, Critias, Sophistes, Philebus,* and *Laws.* Plato died at the age of eighty while attending a wedding banquet in Athens in 347 B.C.

CONTENTS

REVISER'S PREFACE   *xiii*

SYMPOSIUM

Dramatis Personae   **3**

Prologue   **5**

Agathon's Dinner Party   **11**

REVISER'S PREFACE

■ ■ ■

Having the task behind me, I can propose with some seriousness what I did not begin to guess when it still lay ahead of me, namely, that revising someone else's translation of a work of Plato's is not much less work than translating it afresh. That raises the question, Why stick with Jowett's old version at all—why not simply produce a new one? I have consulted many of the translations produced since Jowett, many of them up-to-date in every possible sense, and Jowett's in my judgment remains superior, in the most important respects, to them all. Jowett has a better command not just of English prose style but of English prose styles, and that gives him a great advantage in rendering a work such as the *Symposium,* in which one genius puts on display his versions of the idiosyncratic speaking styles of a group containing two other geniuses, plus a less original third who was ranked in antiquity as the greatest tragic poet after Aeschylus, Sophocles, and Euripides; of the remaining four speakers, one, the drunken Alcibiades, was reckoned by his contemporaries to be the most all-around brilliant member of his generation.

Jowett's successors, especially the more recent ones, are hampered by the contemporary abhorrence of any style other than the spontaneously informal and colloquial (not the same thing as the plain style), though Jowett may sometimes have erred too much in the other direction (see below). Modern tastes seem to coerce modern translators into adopting one or the other of two approaches only: the uniformly casual and colloquial, or the uniformly, and drily, literal—neither approach likely to produce a particularly happy version of the *Symposium.* Jowett, in comparison, had much greater freedom than we have—when Plato's speakers soar, Jowett often succeeds remarkably well in soaring after them, and we can follow along without too much embarrassment: after all, we expect such flights in nineteenth-century writers. Furthermore, I suspect that there are many besides me who actually prefer to think and find that the speech of such personages as Plato here depicts might be more stylish, subtler, richer, and more accomplished than what we are used to hearing from our own friends and selves.

The revisions I have attempted are of two kinds: First, I have incorporated scholarly advances made in the establishment and interpretation of the Greek text since Jowett's time, in which category I include changes imposed where I simply disagree with Jowett's interpretation or think he made a mistake (sometimes Jowett changed the order of sentences, for example; I have tended to restore the order of the original). Second, I have removed archaisms or affectations of or in Jowett's English—those that strike me as likely to strike my contemporaries as ridiculous or, at best, off-puttingly quaint. For example, Jowett's "the tale of love was on this wise" I change to "the tale of love was like this." "What say you to going?" becomes "What do you say to going?" "Please to see to this" becomes "Please see to this." Adjustments of this kind have been made widely and deeply. For example, the opening sentence of the work is rendered by Jowett: "Concerning the things about which you ask to be informed I believe that I am not ill-prepared with an answer." This manages to be both stilted and a little arch in the high Victorian Oxford manner. The Greek, on the other hand, is somewhat informal and quite intimate—we are clearly overhearing a conversation that is already in progress, and is conducted among friends.

Apollodorus uses an idiom that, while not quite diffident, is urbanely removed from the self-assertive: "Actually, it turns out that I am quite well up on the matter you are asking about." That is a fairly radical departure from Jowett's text. It must be emphasized, however, that I have not found the need for such significant tampering to be spread evenly through the work: some passages have been subjected to extensive and deep adjustment; others (for example, much of Alcibiades' speech) have barely been touched.

It will be seen that many of the changes I make comply with changes in taste that have occurred between Jowett's time and our own. That brings us to the question of the handling of sexual matters. Readers may automatically assume that since Jowett was a Victorian, his translation of an ancient Greek work largely devoted, as the *Symposium* is, to the joys (or at least the theoretical joys) of male homosexual love must be full of puritanical euphemisms and bowdlerizations of the frank and uninhibited original text. Jowett is in fact not so prudish, and, more important, the original does not even approach the lewd. It must be granted that when a speaker is referring unambiguously to physical sex acts—for example, a young boy's complying with the sexual initiations of an older male suitor—Jowett says things like "the boy grants his lover this favour," and this may strike us as coy. The fact of the matter, however, is that "grant a favor" is not a bad literal translation of the most characteristic Greek verb used in such contexts, *charizesthai* (cognate with the word from which our "charity" derives). Jowett's version, as it turns out, is misleading, but not because of any lack of literal accuracy: his infidelity to the original is rather a result of situating his literal rendition in an alien cultural context. In Greek the association of *charizesthai* with sexual compliance is so common and consistent that the word is completely unambiguous and hence completely uneuphemistic; in the cultures of both Victorian and present-day English, to refer to sexual submission as "granting a favor" is coy. In such instances as this I have nudged the renderings in the direction of a greater frankness, without, I hope, descending into the inaccurately vulgar. I have, for example, permitted *paederastia* to emerge as either "pederasty" or "boy-love" instead of "the love of youths," which is simply too sanitized. The essential point that has guided my efforts is that the speakers are not leering, or coy, or indecent, but consistently urbane and, in many instances, amusedly detached.

The translation of passages treating of sexual matters naturally invites discussion of the sexual matters themselves. Many readers may be taken aback by some of the assumptions revealed in the characters' talk. Such readers might guess that the persons here depicted by Plato constitute an isolated, specifically homosexual group, such as might be found today gathered in certain types of bars and other establishments, or might generalize to the conclusion that pederasty was a much more open and widespread practice in Classical Greece than in the Western world of today. Both conclusions would be largely wrong, though each contains an element of truth. The evidence certainly does suggest that the average Greek male of the Classical period would be comparatively unsurprised and unimpressed if he detected bisexual impulses in his male acquaintance or even in himself. (There are very few unambiguous references to female homosexuality in the early periods—Aristophanes' speech here contains one of the first—whereas references to male homosexuality, especially with insulting intent in the writings of comic poets such as, again, Aristophanes, are innumerable.) On the other hand, however common it may have been thought to be, the homosexual impulse certainly does not seem to have been accorded blanket approval or admiration by the preponderance of Athenian citizens (to confine ourselves to the best-documented community). For example, we often see the imputation of such impulses or activities deployed as a way of ridiculing or insulting a person. In sum, it seems about right to say that the culture of the period, if it did not *accept* homosexuality quite so warmheartedly as some modern advocates have hoped, nonetheless did *expect* homosexual impulses and acts to exist and occur to a greater degree than present-day Western cultures have tended to. The characters of the *Symposium* appear, in the aggregate, to go even further, and to exhibit an even greater acceptance (to the point of avidity in several cases) of the phenomenon.

That much will do for the background; but it would violate the whole spirit of the *Symposium* to acquiesce to reductive formulations about human sexuality, sexual orientations, and love. That, after all, is the subject of the work, and the work must be allowed to speak for itself and be heard on its own, without too much background chatter from its commentators.

The marginal numbers accompanying the text correspond to the page numbers and subsections (represented by the letters *a* through *e*) of the complete edition of Plato published in Paris by Henri Étienne (= Stephanus) in 1578. This pagination, known as the "Stephanus numbers," is universally used for referring to specific passages in Plato's works; thus, for example, Socrates's major speech in the *Symposium* ends in 212c.

SYMPOSIUM

DRAMATIS PERSONAE

■ ■ ■

APOLLODORUS:
The narrator, who repeats to his
companions the report that he had heard from
Aristodemus, and had already narrated to
Glaucon a few days before.[1]

UNIDENTIFIED COMPANIONS OF APOLLODORUS

ARISTODEMUS

AGATHON

SOCRATES

PAUSANIAS

ARISTOPHANES

ERYXIMACHUS

PHAEDRUS

ALCIBIADES

A CROWD OF UNIDENTIFIED REVELERS

---

[1]One of the most notable features of the form of this work is its "I heard it from X, who heard it from Y" structure; it is difficult for his readers to guess Plato's motives for taking this approach. It is extraordinarily difficult for his translators to harmonize the successive nestings of direct speech, reported speech, reported-reported speech, etc., with the limited resources of English punctuating conventions. My basic solution is as follows: Within the Prologue the exchanges reported by Apollodorus in his recent meeting with Glaucon are put into double quotation marks; once the prologue is over (and we are in Apollodorus' report of what Aristodemus told *him*), double quotation marks are used for the utterances of the participants in the symposium itself.

PROLOGUE

APOLLODORUS:

Actually, it turns out that I am quite well up on the matter 172
you are asking about, since just the other day, when I was
heading for the city from my house in Phalerum, one of my
acquaintances caught sight of me from behind and called
out playfully from a ways off, and said, "O Phalerian one!—
Hey, Apollodorus!—Won't you wait up?" So I stopped and
waited, and he said, "Why, I was looking for you, Apollodorus, only just now, to ask you about the speeches in

b praise of love given by Socrates, Alcibiades, and others, at that dinner party of Agathon's. Phoenix, the son of Philip, told someone else, who told me of them; his account was very unclear, but he said that you knew—so please relate them to me. After all, who better is there to report the words of your friend than you? But first tell me," he said, "were you at the party yourself?"

"Your informant, Glaucon," I said, "must have been very
c unclear indeed, if you imagine that the occasion was recent, or that I could have been a member of the party."

"Well, yes," he replied, "I did have that impression."

"Impossible," I said. "Are you unaware that it has been many years since Agathon has lived in Athens, and not three have elapsed since I became acquainted with Socrates, and have made it my daily business to know all that he says and
173 does? There was a time before then when I used to run about the world, fancying myself to be accomplishing something, but I was really a very miserable person—no better than you are now, in fact: I thought that I ought to do anything rather than be a philosopher."

"Well," he said, "joking apart, tell me when the dinner party took place."

"In our boyhood," I replied, "when Agathon won the prize with his first tragedy, on the day after the one on which he and his chorus offered the victory sacrifice."

"It must have been a really long time ago," he said. "And who told you—did Socrates?"

"Oh no," I replied, "but the same person who told b
Phoenix. He was a little fellow, who never wore any shoes,
Aristodemus, of the deme of Cydathanaeum.[1] He had been
at Agathon's feast, and I think that in those days there was
no one who was a more passionate admirer of Socrates.
Furthermore, I have asked Socrates about the accuracy of
some parts of his narrative, and he confirmed them."

"Then," said Glaucon, "let us have the tale over again;
isn't the journey to Athens just made for conversation?"

And so we walked, and talked of the speeches about
love; and that is how it happens that, as I said at first, I am c
well practiced on this subject, and will now have another
run-through of the speeches if you like. To talk or to hear
others talk of philosophy always gives me the greatest
pleasure, to say nothing of the profit. On the other hand,
when I hear certain other kinds of talk, especially, for example, that of you rich people and businessmen, I am pro-
foundly depressed, and I pity you who are my
companions, because you think that you are doing something when in reality you are doing nothing. I imagine d
that you pity me in return, and think me an unhappy
creature, and very probably you think right. But, you see,
I *know* of you what you only *think* of me—there is the difference.

---

[1]Attica, the territory of Athens, was divided into smaller communities called
demes.

ONE OF APOLLODORUS' PRESENT COMPANIONS:
I see, Apollodorus, that you are just the same: speaking ill always of yourself—and especially of others. I do believe that you pity all mankind, with the exception of Socrates, yourself first of all. How you ever came by your nickname "Tenderheart" I will never understand; for you are always raging, as now, against yourself and everybody but Socrates.

APOLLODORUS:
e Yes, friend, and of course it's obvious that thinking thus about myself and about you, I must be mad or demented; no other evidence is required.

COMPANION:
No more of that, Apollodorus; but let me renew my request that you repeat the conversation.

APOLLODORUS:
Well, the tale of love was like this— But perhaps I had bet-
174 ter begin at the beginning, and try to give you the exact words of Aristodemus.

AGATHON'S
DINNER PARTY

■ ■ ■

Aristodemus said that he met Socrates fresh from the bath, and with sandals on; and as Socrates was only rarely shod, he asked him where he was going that he had been transformed into such a fop.

"To a dinner party at Agathon's," he replied, "whose invitation to his victory sacrifice I refused yesterday, fearing a crowd, but I promised that I would come today instead. And so I have put on my finery, because he is such a fine man. What do you say to going with me without an invitation?" 174b

"I will do as you bid me," I replied.

"Follow then," he said, "and let us demolish the proverb 'To the feasts of inferior men the good unbidden go,' instead of which our proverb will run, 'To the feasts of the good the good unbidden go'.[2] And this alteration may be supported by the authority of Homer himself, who not only demolishes but literally outrages the proverb. For, after picturing Agamemnon as a man exceptionally *good* at war, he makes Menelaus, who is only a fainthearted warrior, come unbidden to the banquet of Agamemnon,[3] who is feasting and offering sacrifices, not the better to the worse, but the worse to the better."

"I am worried, Socrates," said Aristodemus, "that this may still be my case, and that, like Menelaus in Homer, I shall be a mediocrity who 'to the feasts of the brilliant unbidden goes.' But I shall say that I was bidden by you, and then you will have to make an excuse."

" 'Two going together,' " he replied, with the Homeric verse,[4] "one or other of us may invent an excuse along the way. But let's go."

---

[2]Socrates is making a pun on the name Agathon ("Goodman") and the Greek word for "good," *agathos,* as if we should say, "To Goodman's feast good men unbidden go."

[3]*Iliad* 2. 408.

[4]*Iliad* 10. 224.

This was the style of their conversation as they went along. But then as they proceeded, Socrates became lost in thought and started steadily dropping behind, finally urging Aristodemus, who was waiting, to go on before him. When Aristodemus reached the house of Agathon, he found the doors wide open, and a comical thing happened. A slave coming out met him, and led him at once into the dining room, in which the guests were reclining, for the dinner party was about to begin. "Welcome, Aristodemus," said Agathon, as soon as he appeared. "You are just in time to sup with us; if you come on any other matter, put it off and join us, as I was looking for you yesterday to invite you, but I could not find you. But what have you done with Socrates?"

I turned round, but Socrates was nowhere to be seen; and I had to explain that he had been with me a moment before, and that I came by his invitation to the supper.

"You were quite right in coming," said Agathon, "but where is he himself?"

"He was coming along behind me just now," he said, "and I cannot think what has become of him."

"Go and look for him, boy," said Agathon, "and bring him in; and meanwhile, please, Aristodemus, take the place by Eryximachus."

A slave then helped him to wash, and he lay down. Soon another slave came in with an announcement: "Socrates is here, but he has gone up onto the portico of the house next door," he said. "There he stands, and when I call him he refuses to come."

"How strange," said Agathon. "Then you must call him again, and keep calling him."

b   "Let him alone," said my informant. "He has a way of stopping anywhere and abstracting himself. I am certain that he will soon appear, so do not disturb him."

"Well, if you think so, I will leave him," said Agathon. And then, turning to the slaves, he added, "Let us have supper without waiting for him. Whenever there is no one to give you orders, which I have never done, you always serve up whatever you please. So now imagine that you are our hosts, and that I and the company are your guests; treat us

c   well, and then we shall commend you."

After this, supper was served, but still no Socrates; and during the meal Agathon several times expressed a wish to send for him, but Aristodemus objected; and at last when the feast was about half over—for the fit, as usual, was not of long duration—Socrates entered. Agathon, who was reclining alone at the end of the table, begged that he would take the place next to him, that "I may touch you," he said,

d   "and have the benefit of that wise thought which came into your mind in the portico, and is now in your possession; for I am certain that you would not have come away until you had found what you sought."

"How I wish," said Socrates, sitting down on the couch,

"that wisdom could be infused by touch, out of the fuller into the emptier man, as water runs siphoned on a string of wool out of a fuller cup into an emptier one; if that were so, how greatly I would value the privilege of reclining at e your side. For you would fill me full with a stream of wisdom plenteous and fair; whereas my own is without a doubt of a very slight and even illusory sort, like a dream. But yours is bright and full of promise, and shone forth in all the splendor of youth the day before yesterday, in the presence of more than thirty thousand Hellenes."

"Don't be cruel, Socrates," said Agathon. "Before long you and I will have to settle the question who bears off the palm of wisdom—of this Dionysus shall be the judge. But at present you are better occupied with supper."

Socrates reclined, and supped with the rest; and then li- 176 bations were offered, and after a hymn had been sung to the god, and there had been the usual ceremonies, they were about to commence drinking, when Pausanias said, "And now, my friends, how can we drink with least injury to ourselves? I can assure you that I feel severely the effect of yesterday's drinks, and need a respite; and I suspect that most of you are in the same predicament, since you were at the party yesterday. Consider then: What would be the least injurious approach to drinking?" b

"I entirely agree," said Aristophanes, "that we should, by all means, avoid hard drinking, for I was myself one of those who were yesterday drowned in drink."

"I think that you are right," said Eryximachus, the son of Acumenus, "but I should still like to hear one other person speak: Is Agathon able to drink hard?"

"I am not up to it," said Agathon.

c "Then," said Eryximachus, "the weak heads, like myself, Aristodemus, Phaedrus, and others who never can drink, are fortunate in finding that the stronger ones are not in a drinking mood. (I do not include Socrates, who is able either to drink heavily or to abstain, and will not mind, whichever we do.) Well, as none of the company seems disposed to drink much, perhaps I will be forgiven for saying,

d as a physician, that heavy drinking is a bad practice, which I never follow, if I can help it, and certainly do not recommend to others, least of all to anyone who still feels the effects of yesterday's carouse."

"I always do what you advise, and especially what you prescribe as a physician," responded Phaedrus of the deme Myrrhinus, "and the rest of the company, if they are wise, will do the same."

e It was agreed that drinking was not to dominate the evening's activities, but that they were all to drink only so much as they pleased.

"Then," said Eryximachus, "as you are all agreed that drinking is to be voluntary, and that there is to be no coercive toasting or the like, I move, in the next place, that the flute-girl, who has just made her appearance, be told to go away and play to herself, or, if she likes, to the women within. Today let us have conversation instead; and, if you will allow me, I will tell you what sort of conversation."

This proposal having been accepted, Eryximachus pro- 177 ceeded as follows:

"I will begin," he said, "after the manner of Melanippe in Euripides, 'Not mine the word' which I am about to speak, but that of Phaedrus.[5] For often he says to me in an indignant tone: 'What a strange thing it is, Eryximachus, that, whereas other gods have poems and hymns made in their honor, so venerable and great a god as Love has not even one encomiast among all the poets, who are so many. b There are the worthy sophists too—the excellent Prodicus, for example—who have descanted in prose on the virtues of Heracles and other heroes. That is not all that amazing, but I have come across a philosophical work of which salt was the subject, and was given extraordinary encomiums for its usefulness; and you could find many other equally c worthy things have had equal honor bestowed upon them. And to think that there should be eager interest in such things as these, and yet to this day no one has ever undertaken to hymn Love in a manner worthy of him! *That* is how utterly this great deity has been neglected.'

"Now in this Phaedrus seems to me to be quite right, and therefore I want to offer him a contribution; further-

---

[5]From Euripides' play *Melanippe the Wise*, which survives only fragmentarily.

more, on this occasion I cannot think of anything better suited to those present than to honor the god Love. If you agree with me, there will be no lack of conversation; for I mean to propose that each of us in turn, going from left to right, shall make as fair a speech as he can in honor of Love, and Phaedrus, because he is sitting first on the left hand, and because he is the father of the proposal, shall begin."

"No one will vote against you, Eryximachus," said Socrates. "How, for example, could *I* oppose your motion, I, who profess to understand nothing but matters of love;[6] nor, I imagine, will Agathon and Pausanias;[7] and there can be no doubt of Aristophanes, whose sole concern is with

---

[6]Does Socrates profess to understand nothing but "matters of love" (i.e., the emotion) or "matters of Love" (i.e., the god)? And what is the difference? Greek thought seems to have flowed more easily than ours between an abstract and its personification (eros and Eros, love and Love), and the writing system, lacking a lower-case alphabet, did not force any decision between "love" and "Love." In the translation I have tried to use "love" where the abstract emotion seems meant, and "Love" for the personified deity, but it will be clear to readers, especially in the speeches of Pausanias and Eryximachus, that the decision for one or the other sometimes fails to do justice to the subtle modulations in the speakers' usages.

[7]There are at least two couples present at the party: Eryximachus is the lover of the younger Phaedrus, and Pausanias of the younger Agathon. The latter relationship was unusual for ancient Athens in that it did not, as was the norm for love affairs between younger and older males, coexist with heterosexual marriage (of the older partner, called the lover, as opposed to the younger, the beloved), but appears to have been the primary relationship of both participants, and continued (again anomalously) after the younger

Dionysus and Aphrodite; nor will anyone else of those whom I see around me disagree. The proposal, as I am aware, seems rather hard upon us whose place is last; but we shall be contented if we hear some good speeches first. Let Phaedrus begin the praise of Love, and good luck to him."

All the company expressed their assent, and urged him to do as Socrates suggested.

■ ■ ■

Now, Aristodemus did not recollect all that each speaker 178 said, and I do not recollect all that he himself related to me; but I will tell you what of the things said by the chief speakers I thought was most worthy of remembrance.

■ ■ ■

Phaedrus began with an argument to the effect that Love is a mighty god and an object of wonder and admiration among gods and men for many different reasons, but especially for his birth. "For he is the eldest of the gods, which is a source of honor to him; and a proof of his claim to this b honor is that there is no record of his parents; no poet or

---

partner had left boyhood far behind. As we see on the present occasion, Agathon, still jocularly referred to by his companions as a "boy" or "lad," is a full-grown adult who has written successful dramas. It is reported that when Agathon left Athens for Macedonia, Pausanias went with him.

prose writer has ever affirmed that he had any. As Hesiod says:[8]

> First Chaos came, and then broad-bosomed Earth,
> The everlasting seat of all that is,
> And Love.

"And Acusilaus agrees with Hesiod. Also Parmenides says about his birth, 'First of all the gods was Love devised.'[9] Thus there are numerous witnesses who acknowledge Love to be the eldest of the gods. And not only is he the eldest, he is also the source of the greatest benefits to us. For I know no greater blessing to a young man who is beginning life than a virtuous lover, or to a lover than a beloved youth. For the principle that ought to be the lifelong guide of men who wish to live nobly—that principle, I say, neither kinship ties, nor honor, nor wealth, nor anything else is able to implant so well as love. Of what principle am I speaking? Of the sense of honor and dishonor, without which neither states nor individuals ever do any good or great work. And I say that a lover who is detected in doing any dishonorable act, or submitting through cowardice when any dishonor is done to him by another, will be more pained at being detected by his beloved than at being seen

---

[8]Hesiod, *Theogony* 116–120, with omissions.

[9]Literally, "X devised Eros first of all the gods"; X, the subject of the verb, is not known, so I have resorted to the passive.

by his father, or by his companions, or by anyone else. The beloved, too, when he is found in any disgraceful situation, e has the same feeling about his lover. And if there were only some way of contriving that a state or an army should be made up of lovers and their loves, they would be the very best governors of their own city, abstaining from all dishonor, and emulating one another in honor; and when fighting at each other's side, although a mere handful, they 179 would overcome the world. For a lover would prefer for all mankind to see him abandon his post or throw away his arms than that his beloved should see him do such things. He would be ready to die a thousand deaths rather than endure that. Then again, who would desert his beloved or fail him in the hour of danger? No one is so cowardly that Love could not inspire him to heroism, equal to that of the bravest, at such a time. That courage which, as Homer says, b the god breathes into the souls of some heroes, Love infuses from his own nature into the lover.

"And as for dying on someone else's behalf—only lovers consent to do this, not only men, but even women. Of this, Alcestis, the daughter of Pelias, is a monument to all Hellas; for she was willing to lay down her life on behalf of her husband, when no one else would, although he had a father and mother; but because of her love she so far exceeded c them in devotion that she made them seem to be strangers in blood to their own son, and related to him in name only. So noble did this action of hers appear to the gods, as well as to men, that among the many who have done noble deeds, she is one of the very few to whom, in admiration for her magnificent act, they have granted the privilege of d returning alive to earth; that is how exceedingly great is the honor paid by the gods to the devotion and virtue of love. But Orpheus, the son of Oeagrus, the harper, they sent away empty-handed, and presented to him only an apparition of her whom he sought, but herself they would not give up, because he showed no spirit; he was only a harp player and did not dare, like Alcestis, to die for love, but was scheming how he might enter Hades alive. Moreover, they afterward caused him to suffer death at the hands of women, as the punishment of his cowardliness, whereas, e very differently, they honored Achilles, the son of Thetis, and sent him to the Isles of the Blest, because, though he had learned from his mother that he would die if he killed Hector, but if he did not, he would return home and live to a good old age, he dared nonetheless to go to the aid of his lover, Patroclus, and, after avenging him, not merely to 180 die on his lover's behalf but to follow him in death. And the gods, overawed by this deed, honored him exceptionally, because his zeal on behalf of his lover was so exceptional. (Aeschylus, incidentally, talks rubbish in saying that Achilles was the lover, Patroclus the beloved; for Achilles was more beautiful not only than Patroclus but than all the other heroes, and as Homer informs us, he was still beardless and younger by far.) And greatly as the gods honor a lover's

love, still, since the lover is more divine (seeing that he is in- b
spired by god), the return of love on the part of the beloved
to the lover is more admired and valued and rewarded by
them. Wherefore the gods honored Achilles even above the
lover Alcestis, and sent him to the Islands of the Blest.

"These are my reasons for affirming that Love is the eldest and noblest and mightiest of the gods, and the chiefest
author and giver of virtue and happiness to men, both in
life and after death."

This, or something like this, was the speech of Phaedrus. c
Some other speeches followed, which Aristodemus did not
remember; the next that he repeated was that of Pausanias:

"Phaedrus," he said, "the argument has not been set before us, I think, quite in the right form: we should not be
called upon to praise Love in such an indiscriminate manner. If there were only one Love, then what you said would
be well enough; but since there are more Loves than one,
you should have begun by determining which of them was
to be the theme of our praises. I will amend this defect; d
and first of all I will tell you which Love is deserving of
praise, and then I will try to formulate my praise in a manner worthy of the god.

"We all know that Love is inseparable from Aphrodite,
and if there were only one Aphrodite, there would be only
one Love; but as there are two Aphrodites, there must be
two Loves. And am I not right in asserting that there are
two Aphrodites? The elder one, having no mother, who is

called the heavenly Aphrodite—she is the daughter of Uranus;[10] the younger, who is the daughter of Zeus and Dione—her we call common, and the Love who is her fellow worker is rightly named common, as the other Love is called heavenly.

"It is axiomatic that all the gods must be praised, and in doing so in this case I must try to state the provinces and prerogatives of the two Loves. Now, the nature of any action—that is, whether it is good or bad—varies according to the manner of its performance. Take, for example, what we are now doing—drinking, singing, and talking; these actions are not in themselves either good or evil, but they turn out in this or that way according to the mode of performing them, and when well done they are good, and when wrongly done they are evil. And in like manner not every kind of love, or rather, not every kind of Love, but only that which has a noble purpose, is noble and worthy of praise. The Love who is the offspring of the common Aphrodite is essentially common, and does whatever presents itself. This Love is the one that the more vulgar sort of men feel, and such men are apt to love women no less than boys, and the bodies of those whom they crave rather than their souls, so they aim for those who are as empty-

---

[10]Uranus—in Greek not a planet, but the heavens conceived as a god, contrasted and partnered with Earth; hence, Aphrodite, daughter of Uranus, is "heavenly Aphrodite."

headed as possible, since they look only toward bringing
the deed off and do not care if they do so honorably or oth-
erwise—for which reason it inevitably turns out that they
do whatever opportunity offers, good, and, just as happily,
ill. The goddess who is the mother of this Love is far
younger than the other, and she was born of the union of c
the male and female, and partakes of both. But the offspring
of the heavenly Aphrodite is derived from a mother in
whose birth the female has no part—she is from the male
only; this is that Love which is of youths, and the goddess
being older, there is nothing of wantonness in her. Those
who are inspired by this Love turn to the male, delighting
in the more valiant and intelligent nature. Anyone may recognize the pure enthusiasts of this Love in the very nature
of their pederasty. For they love not little boys but intelli- d
gent beings whose reason is beginning to be developed,
about the time at which their beards begin to grow. And in
choosing young men to be their companions, they mean to
be faithful to them and pass their whole life in company
with them, not to take them in their juvenile inexperience,
and deceive them, and then abandon them with ridicule, to
run off with another. But the love of little boys should be
forbidden by law, because their future is uncertain; they e
may turn out good or bad, either in body or soul, and much
serious effort may be thrown away upon them. In this matter the good are a law to themselves, and the coarser sort of
lovers ought to be restrained by force, as we restrain or at-

tempt to restrain them from fixing their affections on
182 women of free birth. These are the persons who bring a reproach on love, with the result that some people have the
nerve to claim that it is disgraceful to grant sexual gratifi-
cation to lovers. They say this looking at the vulgar type,
observing their impropriety and lawlessness—for surely
nothing that is decorously and lawfully done can justly be
censured?

"Now, here and in Lacedaemon the rules about love are
perplexing, but in most cities they are simple and easily in-
b telligible. In Elis and Boeotia, and in countries having no
gifts of eloquence, they are very straightforward; the law is
simply that gratifying lovers is a noble thing to do, and no
one, whether young or old, has anything to say to the
lovers' discredit, the reason being, as I suppose, that they are
men of few words in those parts, and therefore the lovers
do not like the trouble of pleading their suit.

"In as many parts of Ionia and other places as are subject
to the barbarians, the custom is held to be dishonorable; love
affairs with youths share the evil repute in which philosophy and gymnastics are held, because they are inimical to
c tyranny; for the interests of rulers require that their subjects
should be weak in spirit, and that there should be no strong
bond of friendship or society among them, which love,
above all other motives, is likely to inspire, as our Athenian
tyrants learned by experience; for the love of Aristogeiton

and the constancy of Harmodius had a strength which undid their power.[11] And, therefore, where illegality and shame have been attached to the act of gratifying lovers, the responsibility is to be ascribed to the evil condition of those who make the laws; that is to say, to the self-seeking of the governors and the cowardice of the governed. On the other hand, the indiscriminate honor that is given to this act in some countries is attributable to the spiritual sloth of the lawmakers.

"In our own country a far better principle prevails, but, as I was saying, the explanation of it is rather perplexing. For observe that open loves are held to be more honorable than secret ones, and that the love of the noblest and highest, even if their persons are less beautiful than others, is especially honorable. Consider, too, how great is the encouragement given by all to the lover—not only is he not thought to be doing anything dishonorable, but if he succeeds he is praised, and if he fail he is blamed! And the custom of our city grants that in the pursuit of his love he be praised for doing many strange things, which would gar-

---

[11]According to Athenian popular belief, the regime of the Peisistratids fell at the end of the sixth century as a result of the assassination of Hipparchus, who was in fact only the brother of the ruling tyrant, Hippias. The assassins were Harmodius and his lover Aristogeiton, seeking to prevent and punish Hipparchus' erotic pursuit of Harmodius.

ner bitter censure if he should dare to do them pursuing
183 and trying to bring off any consummation other than this
one. For if, from any motive of financial interest or wish for
office or power, he should be willing to do what lovers do
in pursuit of their darlings—pray, and entreat, and suppli-
cate, and swear oaths, and sleep outside the beloved's door,
and voluntarily endure a slavery worse than that of any
slave—in any other case his friends and enemies alike
would be ready to prevent him; but in the case of love there
b is no friend who will be ashamed of him and admonish
him, and no enemy will charge him with servility or flattery. There is an ennobling charm to a lover doing all these
things, and it is granted by custom that he do them without censure, since he is trying to accomplish something
magnificent. And what is strangest of all, the lover alone
may swear and forswear himself (so men say), and the gods
will forgive his transgression, for they say that a lover's oath
c is not binding. Such is the entire liberty that gods and men
have allowed the lover, according to the custom that prevails in our part of the world. From this point of view a
man might suppose that in Athens to be a lover and to be
a lover's 'friend' is held to be a very honorable thing. But
when their fathers forbid the beloveds to talk with their
lovers, and place them under the care of a tutor, who is ap-
pointed to see to these things, and their companions and
coevals cast in their teeth anything of the sort that they may
d observe to happen, and their elders refuse to silence the re-

provers and do not rebuke them for rudeness—anyone who reflects on all this will, on the contrary, think that we hold these practices to be most disgraceful. But, as I was saying at first, the truth, as I imagine, is that the matter is not a straightforward one. Such practices are in and of themselves neither honorable nor dishonorable; rather, they are honorable when done honorably, dishonorable when done dishonorably. There is dishonor in yielding to the base, or in a base manner; but there is honor in yielding to the good, or in an honorable manner. Base is that vulgar lover who loves the body rather than the soul, inasmuch as e he is not even stable, because he loves a thing that is in it-self unstable, and therefore when the bloom of youth that he was desiring is over, he 'takes wing and flies away,'[12] dis-honoring all his words and promises; whereas the lover with the noble disposition is constant for life, because he becomes one with the everlasting. The custom of our country would have both of them proven well and truly, 184 and would have the beloved yield to the one sort of lover and avoid the other, and therefore encourages lovers to pursue, and beloveds to flee, testing both the lover and beloved in contests and trials until they show to which of the two classes they respectively belong. And this is the rea-son why, in the first place, a hasty surrender is held by cus-tom to be dishonorable, because time is the true test of this

---

[12]*Iliad* 2. 71.

as of most other things; and secondly, there is dishonor in being overcome by the love of money, or of wealth, or of

b political power, whether a man is frightened into surrender by the loss of them, or, having experienced the benefits of money and political corruption, is unable to rise above the seductions of them. For none of these things is of a permanent or lasting nature; not to mention that no generous friendship ever sprang from them. There remains, then, according to our custom, only one path by which a beloved might honorably gratify his lover; for, as we saw that our custom allows that any service that the lover does for his

c beloved is not to be accounted flattery or be reviled, so the beloved has one way only of voluntary service that is not a source of censure, and this is the service of virtue.

"For we have a custom, and according to our custom anyone who does service to another under the idea that he will be improved by him, either in wisdom or in some other particular of virtue—such a voluntary service, I say, is not to be regarded as a dishonor, and is not open to the charge of flattery. And these two customs, the one concerned with boy-love, and the other with the practice of

d philosophy and virtue in general, ought to meet in one, and then the beloved may honorably indulge the lover. For when the lover and beloved come together, having each of them a law, and the lover thinks that he is right in doing any service that he can to his compliant beloved, and the other that he is right in submitting to any service that he can for him who is making him wise and good, the one capable of communicating intelligence and virtue, the other seeking e to acquire them with a view to education and wisdom; when the two laws of love are fulfilled and meet in one— then, and then only, may the beloved yield with honor to the lover. Nor when love is of this disinterested sort is there any disgrace in being deceived, but in every other case there is equal disgrace in being or not being deceived. For he who is gracious to his lover under the impression that 185 he is rich, and is disappointed of his gains because he turns out to be poor, is disgraced all the same: for he has done his best to show that he would give himself up to anyone's 'uses base' for the sake of money, and this is not honorable. And on the same principle if someone should give himself to a lover because he seems a good man, and in the hope that he will be improved by his company, and should in the end be deceived, even though the object of his affection turn out to be a villain, and to have no virtue, still, the error is a b noble one. For he too has shown his true nature, that for the sake of virtue and improvement he will eagerly do anything for anybody, and there can be nothing nobler than this.

"Thus it is noble in every case to gratify another for the sake of virtue. This is that love which is the Love of the heavenly goddess, and is heavenly, and of great value to individuals and cities, making the lover and the beloved alike eager in the work of their own improvement. But all other

c loves are the offspring of the other, who is the common
goddess.

"To you, Phaedrus, I offer this my contribution in praise
of Love, which is as good as I could make extempore."

Pausanias came to a pause—this is the balanced way in
which I have been taught by the experts to speak;[13] and
Aristodemus said that the turn of Aristophanes was next,
but either because he had eaten too much, or from some
other cause, he had the hiccoughs and was obliged to
d change turns with Eryximachus, the physician, who was reclining on the couch below him. "Eryximachus," he said,
"you ought either to stop my hiccoughs, or to speak in my
turn until I have gotten rid of them."

"I will do both," said Eryximachus: "I will speak in your
turn, and then you speak in mine; and let me recommend

---

[13]The Greek, meaning literally "Pausanias having ceased," runs *Pausaniou de
pausamenou,* and forms a symmetrical rhythmic pattern. Word play and
rhythmical balance ("the balanced way in which I have been taught by the
experts to speak") were the distinctive features of the style of the sophist
Gorgias of Leontini, closely imitated by, among others, the historical
Agathon, as shown in his surviving fragments, and by the Platonic Agathon
in his speech later on in the *Symposium.* Because he was a sophist, Gorgias
and all his works were for Plato objects of intense suspicion, as readers of
the dialogue *Gorgias* will know. As to the pleasantry in the text above ("Pausanias came to a pause"), it is worth remarking that this is one of the few
places in which our narrator, Apollodorus, makes something resembling an
editorial intervention; its exact significance, if it has any beyond sheer play-
fulness, is hard to gauge.

that while I am speaking you hold your breath, and if after you have done so for some time the hiccough is no better, then gargle with a little water; and if it still continues, tickle ℇ your nose with something and sneeze; and if you sneeze once or twice, even the most violent hiccoughs are sure to go away." "I will do as you prescribe," said Aristophanes, "and now get on with your speech."

Eryximachus spoke as follows:

"Seeing that Pausanias made a fair beginning, but only a lame ending, I must endeavor to supply his deficiency. I 186 think that he has rightly distinguished two kinds of love. But my art further informs me that the double love is not an affection toward the beautiful found exclusively in the soul of man but is to be found, with a multitude of different objects, elsewhere besides—in the bodies of all animals, for example, and in productions of the earth, and I may say in all that is; such is the conclusion that I am convinced I have seen supported from my own art of medicine, namely, that the deity of love is great and wonderful and universal, ♭ and his empire extends over all things, divine as well as human. And I will begin my speech with medicine in order that I may do honor to my art.

"It is in the nature of human bodies that they comprise the two types of love. For it is agreed that in bodily terms that which is healthy and that which is diseased are different and unlike, and furthermore that unlike things desire and love unlike objects; it follows that the love in the healthy is one thing, and that in the diseased is different. Just as Pausanias has said, that to gratify good men is honorable,

c and licentious men dishonorable, so too it stands in the case of the body that it is noble and necessary to gratify the good and healthy elements—and this is what has the name of medicine—and the bad elements and the elements of disease are not to be indulged but to be discouraged, if someone is going to prove to be a truly expert practitioner. For medicine may be regarded generally as the knowledge of the loves and desires of the body and how to satisfy them

d or not; and the best physician is he who is able to separate fair love from foul, or to convert one into the other; and he who knows how to eradicate and how to implant love, whichever is required, is a skillful practitioner. For it is necessary that he be able to reconcile the most hostile elements in the constitution and make them loving friends. Now, the most hostile are the most opposite, such as hot and cold, bitter and sweet, moist and dry, and the like. It was thanks

e to his knowing how to implant love—that is, accord—in these elements that my ancestor, Asclepius,[14] created our art, as our friends the poets here tell us, and I believe them.

"Now, not only medicine in every branch, but the arts of gymnastic and husbandry are governed by the god Love.

---

[14]Asclepius, son of Apollo and the legendary inventor of medical art, is claimed by Eryximachus as an "ancestor," presumably in the sense that as a doctor, Eryximachus (like all doctors) is Asclepius' heir.

Anyone who pays the least attention to the subject will also 187
perceive that in music there is the same reconciliation of
opposites; and I suppose that this must have been the meaning of Heraclitus, although his words are not accurate; for
he says that 'The One is united by disunion, like the harmony of the bow and the lyre.' There is an absurdity in saying that harmony is discord or is composed of elements
that are still in a state of discord. But what he probably
meant was that harmony is composed of differing notes of
higher or lower pitch, which disagreed once but are now b
reconciled by the art of music; for if the higher and lower
notes still disagreed, there would be no harmony—clearly
not. For harmony is symphony, and symphony is an agreement; but there cannot be an agreement of disagreements
so long as they disagree; that which disagrees cannot harmonize. Similarly, rhythm is compounded of elements short
and long, once differing and now in accord. And as in the c
former instance, medicine, so in all these other cases, it is
music that implants this accord, making love and unison to
grow up among them; and thus music, too, is knowledge of
the principles of love in their application to harmony and
rhythm. Again, in the essential nature of harmony and
rhythm there is no difficulty in discerning love that has not
yet become double. But when you want to use them in actual life, either in the composition of songs or in the cor- d
rect performance of tunes or meters composed already,
which latter is called education, then the difficulty begins,

and the good artist is needed. It is the same story all over again: one must gratify those men who are orderly, in such a way that those who are not yet orderly may become so, and to preserve the love of these orderly men—this is that

e noble and heavenly love, the Love of Urania the muse. And again, there is the common Love, that of Polyhymnia, which a person must apply, to whomever he applies it, cautiously, in order that the pleasure be enjoyed but may not generate licentiousness; just as in my own art it is a great matter so to regulate the desires of the epicure that he may gratify his tastes without the attendant evil of disease. Whence I infer that in music, in medicine, in all other things human as well as divine, both Loves ought to be noted as far as may be, for they are both present.

188 "The course of the yearly seasons is also full of both these principles; and when, as I was saying, the elements of hot and cold, moist and dry, attain the orderly Love of one another and blend in temperance and harmony, they bring to men, animals, and plants health and plenty, and do them no harm; whereas the wanton Love, getting the upper hand and affecting the seasons of the year, is very destructive and

b injurious, being the source of pestilence, and bringing many other kinds of diseases on animals and plants; for hoarfrost and hail and blight spring from the excesses and disorders of these elements of love, the knowledge of which, in relation to the revolutions of the heavenly bodies and the seasons of the year, is termed astronomy. Furthermore all sacrifices and the whole province of divination, which is the art of communion between gods and c men—these, I say, are concerned only with the preservation of the good and the cure of the evil Love. For all manner of impiety is likely to ensue if, instead of accepting and honoring and reverencing the harmonious Love in all his actions, a man honors the other Love, whether in his feelings toward gods or parents, toward the living or the dead. Wherefore the business of divination is to see to these Loves and to heal them, and divination is the peacemaker of gods and men, working by a knowledge of the religious d or irreligious tendencies that exist in human loves.

"Such generally is the great and mighty, or rather omnipotent force of Love. And the Love, more especially, that is concerned with the good and is realized in company with temperance and justice, whether among gods or men, has the greatest power, and is the source of all our happiness and harmony, and makes it possible for us to be friends with the gods, who are above us, and with one another.

"I dare say that I too have omitted several things that might be said in praise of Love, but this was not intentional, e and you, Aristophanes, may now supply the omission or take some other line of commendation; for I perceive that you are rid of the hiccoughs."

"Yes," said Aristophanes, who followed, "the hiccoughs 189 did stop, not, however, until I applied the sneezing, and I wonder whether the 'orderly' part of the body has a love of such noises and ticklings as go into a sneeze, for I no sooner applied the sneezing than I was cured."

Eryximachus said: "Beware, my friend Aristophanes; by starting your speech with such pleasantries you compel me to stand guard over it, looking out to see if you will say something derisive—though you *could* speak without disturbing the peace between us."

"You are quite right," said Aristophanes, laughing. "I will unsay my words, and please do not stand guard over me, as I fear that during the speech I am about to make, instead of others laughing with me, which would be all to the good and appropriate to my particular muse, I shall only be laughed at by them."

"Do you expect to shoot your bolt and escape, Aristophanes? Well, perhaps if you are very careful and bear in mind that you will be called to account, I may be induced to let you off."

"In fact, Eryximachus, I intend to take a different line from that taken by you and Pausanias. For it seems to me that mankind has never at all understood the power of Love, since if they had understood him, they would surely have built noble temples and altars, and would offer solemn sacrifices in his honor; but this is not done, and most certainly ought to be done, since of all the gods he is the best friend of men, the helper and the healer of the ills that are the great impediment to the happiness of the race. I will therefore try to initiate you into the mysteries of his power, and you shall be the instructors of others.

"In the first place, let me treat of man's native constitution and its sufferings—for our original constitution was not like the present, but was different. The sexes were three in number, not, as they are now, two, male and female; there was also as a third the union of the two, having a name corresponding to this double nature, which had once a real existence, but is now lost, and the word 'androgynous' is preserved only as a term of reproach. In the second place, the primeval man was round, his back and sides forming a circle; and he had four hands and four feet, one head with two faces, looking opposite ways, set on a round neck and precisely alike; also four ears, two sets of genitals, and the remainder to correspond. He could walk upright as men now do, backwards or forwards as he pleased, and he could also roll over and over at a great pace, pushing off with his four hands and four feet, eight in all, like tumblers going over and over with their legs in the air; this was when he wanted to run fast. Now, the sexes were three, and such as I have described them, because the sun, moon, and earth are three; and the man was originally the child of the sun, the woman of the earth, and the man-woman of the moon, which is made up of sun and earth, and they were all round and moved round and round like their parents.

"Terrible was their might and strength, and the thoughts

of their hearts were great, and they made an attack upon the gods; the tale told by Homer of Otys and Ephialtes actually refers to the original humans: they dared to scale heaven, and would have laid hands upon the gods.[15] Doubt reigned in the celestial councils. Should they kill them and annihilate the race with thunderbolts, as they had done the giants? But then there would be an end of the sacrifices and worship that men offered to them. On the other hand, how could the gods suffer their insolence to go unchecked? At last, after a good deal of reflection, Zeus discovered a way. He said: 'I think I've found a plan that will humble their pride and improve their manners: men shall continue to exist, but I will cut them in two, and then they will be diminished in strength and increased in numbers; this will have the advantage of making them more profitable to us. They shall walk upright on two legs, and if they continue to be insolent and will not be quiet, I will split them again and they shall hop about on a single leg.' He spoke and cut men in two, like a sorb apple that is halved for pickling, or as you might divide an egg with a hair; and as he cut them one after another, he ordered Apollo to give the face and the remaining half of the neck a turn in order that the man might contemplate the dissection of himself (he would thus learn a lesson of humility), and to heal the rest of his wounds, too. So Apollo gave the face a turn and pulled the

---

[15] *Iliad* 5. 385ff.

skin from the sides all over what is now called the belly, and he made one mouth at the center, which he fastened, like a drawstring purse, with a knot (the same which is called the navel); he also molded the chest and took out most of 191 the wrinkles, using a tool like that used by a shoemaker smoothing leather upon a last; he left a few, however— those in the region of the belly around the navel—to be a memorial of this primeval suffering.

"After the division the two parts of man, each yearning for his other half, came together, and, throwing their arms about each other, and intertwining in mutual embraces out of a desire to grow into one, they started dying off from hunger and self-neglect, because they did not like to do b anything apart; and when one of the halves died and the other survived, the survivor sought another mate, man or woman, as we call them—being the sections of entire men or women—and clung to that. They were being destroyed, when in pity of them Zeus devised a new plan: he turned their genitals around to the front, for this had not always been their position, and they sowed the seed no longer, as hitherto, like grasshoppers in the ground, but in one an- c other; and he effected this transposition, and caused the male to generate in the female, in order that their mutual embraces might be procreative, in the case of man joining woman, and that thus the race be continued, or, if male came to male, that they might at least derive satisfaction from the coition, and rest, and go their ways to the business

of life: so ancient is the desire for one another that is im-
d planted in us, reuniting our original nature, trying to make
one of two, and healing the state of man. Each of us, sliced
in two like a flat fish, is but the half of a man—from one,
two. And each is always looking for his other half.

"Now men who are a section of that double nature that
was once called androgynous are lovers of women; adulter-
e ers are generally of this breed, and also adulterous women
who lust after men.

"Women who are a section of the woman do not care
for men, but are more inclined toward women: lesbians
spring from this type.

"Finally, those who are a section of the male pursue the
male, and while they are young, being slices of the original
man, they love men and enjoy lying down with and inter-
192 mingling with men, and they are themselves the best of
boys and youths, because they have the most manly nature.
Some indeed assert that they are shameless, but this is not
true; for they do not act thus from any want of shame, but
because they are valiant and manly, and have a manly coun-
tenance, and they embrace that which is like them. And
these, when they grow up become politicians, and these
only, which is a great proof of the truth of what I am saying. When they reach manhood they are lovers of youth,
b and are not naturally inclined to marry or beget children—
if at all, they do so only in obedience to the law; but they
are satisfied if they may be allowed to live with one another

unwedded; and such a nature is prone to love and ready to return love, always embracing that which is akin to him. And when one of them meets with his other half, the actual half of himself, whether he be a lover of boys or a lover of another sort, the pair are lost in an amazement of love and friendship and intimacy, and one will not be out of the c other's sight, as I may say, even for a moment: these are the people who pass their whole lives together; yet they could not explain what they desire of each other. No one could plausibly think that it is just sexual relations that makes them enjoy each other's company with so much intensity; rather, the soul of each manifests a desire for something else, but what that is it is unable to say, and gives only ob- d scure, oracular pronouncements of its wishes, and makes riddles.

"Now, suppose Hephaestus, with his instruments, were to come to the pair as they are lying side by side and to say to them, 'What do you people want of each other?' They would be unable to explain. And suppose, further, that when he saw their perplexity he said, 'Do you desire to be wholly one, always day and night to be in each other's company? For if this is what you desire, I am ready to fuse and weld you together, so that being two, you shall become e one, and while you live, live a common life as if you were a single man, and after your death in the world below still be one departed soul instead of two—I ask whether this is what you lovingly desire, and whether you are satisfied

with this?' There is not a one of them who, when he heard the proposal, would refuse or prove to want something else, but he would simply think that in this meeting and melting into each other, this becoming one instead of two, he had heard what he now recognized to be the articulation of his long-time yearning. And the reason for this is that the human constitution was originally one and we were a whole, and the desire and pursuit of the whole is called
193 love. There was a time, I say, when we were one, but now because of the wickedness of mankind God has dispersed us, as the Arcadians were dispersed into villages by the Lacedaemonians. And if we are not obedient to the gods, there is a danger that we shall be split up again and go about in bas-relief, like the profile figures having only half a nose that are sculptured on monuments, and that we shall be like tallies.[16] Wherefore let us exhort all men to piety, that we
b may avoid evil and obtain the good, of which Love is to us the lord and minister; and let no one oppose him: whoever opposes him is the enemy of the gods. For if we are friends of the god and at peace with him we shall find our own true loves, which rarely happens in this world at present. I am serious, and therefore I must beg Eryximachus not to

---

[16]A token or tally was an object, typically a knucklebone (used also for dice), that was broken into two asymmetrical pieces that were used for identification: I can securely identify as my (newborn) child the one on whose necklace hangs the tally corresponding to that on mine.

make fun or to find in what I am saying any allusion to Pausanias and Agathon, who, as I suspect, are both of the all-male constitution, and belong to the class I have been c describing. But my words have a wider application—they include men and women everywhere; I believe that if our loves were perfectly accomplished, and each one, restored to his primeval nature, had his original true love, then our race would be happy. And if this would be best of all, the next best under present circumstances must be the nearest approach to such a union; and that will be the attainment of a congenial love. Wherefore, if we would praise him who has given to us the benefit, we must praise the god Love, d who is our greatest benefactor, both leading us in this life back to our own nature, and giving us high hopes for the future, that if we are pious, he will restore us to our original state, and heal us and make us happy and blessed.

"This, Eryximachus, is my discourse of Love, which, although different from yours, I must beg you to leave unassailed by the shafts of your ridicule, in order that each may have his turn; each, or rather either, for Agathon and e Socrates are the only ones left."

"Indeed, I am not going to attack you," said Eryximachus, "for I thought your speech charming, and if I did not know that Agathon and Socrates are masters in the art of love, I should be really afraid that they would have nothing to say, after the world of things that have been said already. But, for all that, I am optimistic."

194   Socrates said: "You performed well when it was your turn, Eryximachus; but if you were in the position I am in now, or rather shall be in when Agathon has spoken, you would, indeed, be very apprehensive, even desperate, as am I."

"You are trying to jinx me, Socrates," said Agathon, "hoping that I will be thrown off by the audience's powerful expectation that I shall speak well."

"I should be strangely forgetful, Agathon," replied
b Socrates, "of the courage and magnificence of spirit you showed when your own compositions were about to be exhibited, and you came upon the stage with the actors and faced the vast theater altogether undismayed, if I thought that your nerves could be fluttered at a small party of friends."[17]

"Do you think, Socrates," said Agathon, "that my head is so full of the theater as not to know how much more formidable to a man of sense a few good judges are than many fools?"

c   "No," replied Socrates, "I should be very wrong to attribute to you, Agathon, that or any other want of refinement. And I am quite aware that if you happened to meet with any whom you thought wise, you would care for their

---

[17]In the *proagon,* held a few days before the dramatic performances, the poets and actors were presented to the public.

opinion much more than for that of the many. But there is no possibility that we here are these wise men you refer to, for we were then in the audience and were a part of the 'many fools'—but I know that if you chanced to be in the presence, not of one of ourselves, but of some really wise man, you would be ashamed of disgracing yourself before him—would you not?"

"Yes," said Agathon.

"But before the many you would not be ashamed, if you thought that you were doing something disgraceful in their presence?"

Here Phaedrus interrupted them, saying: "Do not answer him, my dear Agathon; for if he can only get a partner with whom he can talk, especially a good-looking one, he will no longer care about the completion of our plan. Now I love to hear him talk; but just at present I must not forget the encomium on Love that I have to exact from each one of you. When you and he have paid your tribute to the god, then you may talk."

"Very good, Phaedrus," said Agathon. "I see no reason why I should not proceed with my speech, as I shall have many other opportunities of conversing with Socrates.

"I desire first to speak of how I ought to speak, and then to speak. For the previous speakers, instead of praising the god Love, seem more to have congratulated mankind on the benefits for which the god is responsible; the actual na-

ture of him who has given these gifts, however, no one has
195 stated. But there is only one right way of praising anything,
namely, to explain in detail both the qualities of the subject
and the qualities of those things of which he is the cause.
Thus the correct order for us is: praise Love first for his nature and qualities, then praise his gifts.

"I solemnly aver—if I may say it without impiety or of-
fence—that of all the blessed gods Love is the most blessed
because he is the most beautiful and the best. And he *is* the
most beautiful: for, in the first place, he is the youngest, and
b of his youth he is himself the witness, fleeing out of the way
of age, who is obviously swift, swifter truly than most of us
like. Love has an innate hatred of him and will not come
anywhere near him; but of the young he is, and with the
young he lives—like to like, as the proverb says.

"Now of the things said by Phaedrus about Love there
are many in which I agree with him, but with this I disagree:
he says that Love is older than Iapetus and Kronos. Not so.
c I maintain him to be the youngest of the gods, and young
forever. The ancient doings among the gods of which Hesiod and Parmenides spoke, if they spoke true, were done of
Necessity and not of Love; had Love been in those days,
there would have been no chaining or mutilation of the
gods, or other violence, but peace and sweetness, as there is
now in heaven, since the rule of Love began. Love is young,
then, and in addition to young, tender; he ought to have a

poet like Homer to display his tenderness, as Homer says of d
Ate[18] that she is a goddess and tender (for if 'her feet are
tender,' then she must be tender in her entirety):

> Her feet are tender, for she sets her steps,
> Not on the ground but on the heads of men.[19]

Herein is an excellent proof of her tenderness, that she
walks not upon the hard but upon the soft. Let us adduce a
similar proof of the tenderness of Love; for he walks not e
upon the earth, nor even upon the skulls of men, which are
not so very soft, but in the softest of all that is he walks and
dwells; for it is in the hearts and souls of both gods and men
that he makes his home, though not in every soul without
exception, for where there is hardness of heart he departs,
where there is softness there he settles down; and nestling
always not only with his feet but with his whole body in
the softest of soft places, how can he be other than the softest of all things? Of a truth he is the tenderest as well as the 196
youngest, and in addition he is of flexile form; for if he were
hard and without flexure he could not enfold all things, or
wind his way undiscovered into and out of every soul of
man. And a proof that his form is flexible and well shaped
is his grace, which is universally admitted to be in a special

---

[18]Ate is delusion personified.
[19]*Iliad* 19. 92f.

manner the attribute of Love; ungrace and love are always at war with each other. The fairness of his complexion is indicated by his habitation among the flowers; for he dwells

b not amid bloomless or fading beauties, whether of body or soul or anything else, but in the place of flowers and scents, there he sits and abides.

"Concerning the beauty of the god I have said enough; and yet there remains much more that I might say. Of his virtue I have now to speak: his greatest glory is that he neither does wrong nor is wrong done, to or by any god or man; for he suffers not by force if he suffers; force

c comes not near him, neither when he acts does he act by force. For all men in all things serve him of their own free will, and where there is voluntary agreement, there, as the laws that are the lords of the city say, is justice. And not only is he just but exceedingly temperate, for Temperance is the acknowledged ruler of the pleasures and desires, and no pleasure ever outdoes Love; he is thus their master and they are his servants, and if he is superior to them, then, being superior to all pleasures and desires, he must be temperate indeed. As to courage, 'even Ares, the God of War,

d is no match for him,'[20] for Ares does not have Love, Love has Ares—love of Aphrodite, that is, as the tale goes[21]—and

---

[20]Sophocles, Fragment 256, from his lost play *Thyestes*. Sophocles actually says that Ares is no match for *Necessity,* not Love.

[21]As related in *Odyssey* 8. 266–366.

the possessor is stronger than the possessed. And if he conquers the bravest of all others, he must be himself the bravest. Of the courage and justice and temperance of the god I have spoken, but I have yet to speak of his wisdom; and according to the measure of my ability I must try to do my best. In the first place he is a poet (and here, like Eryximachus, I magnify my art), and he is also the source e of poesy in others, which he could not be if he were not himself a poet. And at the touch of him everyone becomes a poet, even if he had no music in him before; this also is a proof that Love is a good poet and accomplished in all the fine arts; for no one can give to another that which he has not himself, or teach that of which he has no knowledge. Who will deny that the creation of the animals is his 197 doing? Are they not all the products of his special expertise, born and begotten of it? And as to the artists, do we not know that he only of them whom love inspires has the light of fame? He whom Love touches not walks in darkness. The arts of archery and medicine and divination were discovered by Apollo, under the guidance of love and desire; so that he too must be a disciple of Love. And the b Muses learned music, Hephaestus metallurgy, Athene to weave, Zeus to govern gods and men—all at the school of Love. And so the spheres and activities of the gods were established and determined only once Love had come to be among them—obviously, love of beauty, for there is no love of ugliness. In the days of old, as I began by saying, dreadful deeds were done among the gods, for they were ruled by Necessity; but ever since this god was born, every good in heaven and earth has arisen from loving the beautiful.

c   "Therefore, Phaedrus, I say of Love that he is the most beautiful and best in himself, and the cause of what is most beautiful and best in all other things. And it comes upon me to speak in verse and say that the god who makes

> Peace among men, the deep sea's windless calm,
> Pause for tempest, the troubled's hypnic balm

d —this is he who empties men of disaffection and fills them with affection, who makes them to meet together at banquets such as these: in sacrifices, feasts, dances, he is our lord—who sends courtesy and sends away discourtesy, who gives kindness ever and never gives unkindness; the friend of the good, the wonder of the wise, the amazement of the gods; desired by those who have no part in him, and precious to those who have the better part in him; parent of delicacy, luxury, desire, fondness, softness, grace; regardful of the good, regardless of the evil: in every word, work, wish,

e fear—savior, pilot, comrade, helper; cosmic principle for all gods and men, leader best and brightest: in whose footsteps let every man follow, sweetly singing in his honor and joining in that sweet strain with which Love charms the thought of gods and men.

"Such is the speech, Phaedrus, half-playful, yet having a certain measure of seriousness, which, according to my ability, I dedicate to the god."

When Agathon had done speaking, Aristodemus said, 198 there was a general cheer; the young man was thought to have spoken in a manner worthy of himself, and of the god. And Socrates, looking at Eryximachus, said: "Tell me, son of Acumenus, did I fear then a fear not to be feared?[22] Or was I not a true prophet when I said that Agathon would make a wonderful oration, and that I should be left high and dry?"

"The part of the prophecy which concerns Agathon," replied Eryximachus, "appears to me to be true; but not the other part—that you will be left high and dry."

"Why, my dear friend," said Socrates, "must not I or any- b one be helpless who has to speak after he has heard such a rich and varied discourse? It was all marvelous, but I am especially struck with the beauty of the concluding words and expressions—who could listen to them without amazement? As I reflected that I would be able to produce not one utterance even approaching the beauty of these, I

---

[22]With the tortuous formulation "fear a fear not to be feared" Socrates is parodying Agathon's verbal style; compare, for example, from the second-to-last paragraph of Agathon's speech above, "who sends courtesy and sends away discourtesy, who gives kindness ever and never gives unkindness."

would have run away for shame, if I had had some way
c out. For the speech reminded me of Gorgias,[23] so that I
literally had that experience mentioned in Homer: I
feared that in his speech Agathon would send up against
my speech a head of Gorgias, dread rhetorician, and turn
me to stone with speechlessness.[24] And then I perceived
how ridiculous I had been when I consented to take my
d turn with you in praising Love, and said that I was a past
master in matters of Love, when I really had no conception how anything ought to be praised. For in my sim-
plicity I imagined that it was necessary to state the facts
about any given topic for praise, and that this was to be the
groundwork, and from these facts the speaker was to
choose the best and set them forth in the most fitting
manner. And I felt quite proud, thinking that I knew the
nature of true praise and should speak well. Whereas I
now see that all along the right way to praise something
was not that, but rather to attribute to it every species of
e greatness and glory, whether really belonging to it or not,
without regard to truth or falsehood—that was no matter;
for the original proposal seems to have been not that each

---

[23]On Gorgias, see note 13.

[24]Socrates refers to *Odyssey* 11. 633–635, where Odysseus, leaving the un-
derworld, is anxious lest Persephone send up a "head of Medusa the Gorgon, dread monster," which according to tradition turned the beholder into
stone. Socrates substitutes for Homer's "Gorgon" the name of Agathon's
style-master, Gorgias.

of you should really praise Love, but only that you should appear to praise him. And so you attribute to Love every imaginable form of praise that can be gathered anywhere; and you say that 'he is all this,' and 'the cause of all that,' making him appear the most beautiful and best of all to 199 those who know him not, for you cannot impose upon those who know him. And a noble and solemn hymn of praise have you rehearsed. But as I misunderstood the nature of the praise when I said that I would take my turn, I must beg to be absolved from the promise that I made in ignorance: 'My tongue swore, but my heart did not' (as Euripides would say).[25] Let's say good-bye, then, to that approach: for I do not praise in that way; no, indeed, I cannot. But if you wish to hear the truth about Love, I am ready to speak in my own manner, though I will not make myself ridiculous by entering into any b rivalry with you. Say then, Phaedrus, whether you would like to have the truth about Love, spoken in any words and in any order that may happen to come into my mind at the time."

Aristodemus said that Phaedrus and the company urged him to speak in any manner he thought best. "Then," Socrates added, "let me have your permission first to ask Agathon a few more questions, in order that I may get his agreement on some points before I give my speech."

---

[25] *Hippolytus* 612.

c   "I grant the permission," said Phaedrus. "Put your questions." Socrates then proceeded as follows:

"I very much think that you started off your speech in the right way, my dear Agathon, in proposing to describe the nature of Love first and afterward his works—that is a way of beginning which I very much approve. And as you have spoken so eloquently of his nature, may I ask you fur-

d ther, Is Love such a sort of thing as to be of something or somebody, or is it of nothing or nobody? Now, I am not asking if Love is 'of somebody' in a sense of being genealogically derived *from,* or of belonging *to,* some mother or father. And, of course, to ask if Love is erotic love *of,* that is, *for,* a mother or father would be grotesque. But actually that grotesquerie points at the usage I *am* getting at: just as if I should pose this very question about 'father' instead of about Love, I would say, Is a father a father *of* somebody or not? And obviously you would reply, if you were of a mind to reply cooperatively, by saying that a father is a father *of* a son or a daughter. Or am I wrong?"

"You are clearly right," said Agathon.

"And you would say the same of a mother?"

He assented.

e   "Yet let me ask you one more question in order to illustrate my meaning: Is not a brother to be regarded essentially as a brother of something?"

"Certainly," he replied.

"That is, of a brother or sister?"

"Yes," he said.

"And now," said Socrates, "I will ask about Love: Is Love of something or of nothing?"

"Of something, surely," he replied.

"That something of which Love is—precisely *what* it is 200 please remember and save for later; for now only tell me whether Love desires it; that is, does Love desire that something of which Love is?"

"Yes, surely."

"And does he possess, or does he not possess, that which he loves and desires?"

"Probably not, I should say."

"Consider whether 'necessarily' is not rather the word," Socrates said, "instead of your 'probably.' The inference that he who desires something lacks it, and that he does not de- b sire something if he does not lack it, is in my judgment, Agathon, absolutely and necessarily true. What do you think?"

"I agree with you," said Agathon.

"Very good. Would he who is large want to be large, or he who is strong want to be strong?"

"That would be inconsistent with our previous admissions."

"True. For he who *is* anything cannot be in lack of those things which he is?"

"Very true."

"And yet," added Socrates, "if a man being strong wanted

to be strong, or being swift wanted to be swift, or being healthy wanted to be healthy, in that case it might be thought, in connection with these attributes and all such things, that those who *are* such and possess these attributes

c also *want* these attributes which they already possess. I give the example in order that we may avoid misconception. For the possessors of these qualities, Agathon, must be supposed to have their respective advantages at the time, whether they like it or not; and who can want that which he has? Therefore, when a person says, 'I am healthy and want simply to be healthy,' and 'I am rich and want to be rich'—to him we shall reply: 'You, my friend, having wealth

d and health and strength, want to have the continuance of them; for at this moment, whether you choose to or not, you have them. And when you say, "I want that which I have," is not your meaning that you want to have what you now have also in the future?' He must agree with us—must he not?"

"He must," replied Agathon.

"Then," said Socrates, "he desires that these things, preserved for him and supplied to him, be his in the future, which is equivalent to saying that he desires something which is not yet available to him, and which as yet he has not got."

e "Very true," he said.

"Then he and every one who desires, desires that which he has not already, and with which he is not supplied, and which he does not possess, and which he is not, and of which he is in want—these are the sorts of things that love and desire seek?"

"Very true," he said.

"Now then," said Socrates, "let us recapitulate the argument. First, is not Love of something, and, then, is it not of whatever things he is supplied with lack of?"[26]

"Yes," he replied.

201

"This being so, recall what you said in your speech was Love's object. If you wish I will recall it for you: You said that the spheres and activities of the gods were established and determined by love of the beautiful; for there is no love for the ugly. Did you not say something of that kind?"

"Yes," said Agathon.

"Yes, my friend, and the remark was a just one. And if this is true, Love is the love of beauty and not of ugliness?"

He concurred.

"And has not the admission already been made that Love b is of what is lacked and not now possessed?"

"Yes," he said.

"Then Love lacks and does not possess beauty?"

"Necessarily," he replied.

"And would you call that beautiful which wants and does not possess beauty in any way?"

"Certainly not."

---

[26]The Greek is intentionally paradoxical: "lack is in ready supply."

"Then would you still say that Love is beautiful?"

Agathon replied, "I fear that I did not know what I was saying."

c "And yet you made a very good speech, Agathon," replied Socrates. "But there is still one small question that I would like to ask you: Is not the good also beautiful?"

"Yes."

"So if Love lacks the beautiful, and the good is beautiful, then Love also lacks the good."

"Far be it from me to gainsay you, Socrates," said Agathon. "Let us assume that what you say is true."

"Say rather, beloved Agathon, that you cannot refute the truth; for Socrates is easily refuted.

d "And now, taking my leave of you, Agathon, I will rehearse a tale of love that I heard from Diotima of Mantineia, a woman wise in this and in many other kinds of knowledge, who once, before the plague came,[27] effected for the Athenians a ten-year postponement of the disease, through sacrifice. She was my instructress in the art of love, and I shall repeat to you what she said to me, beginning with the points on which Agathon and I agreed, and I shall speak both parts myself as well as I can. As you, Agathon,
e suggested, it is necessary first to give an account of the identity and nature of Love, and then of his works. In view of this it seems to me easiest to proceed in the way the for-

---

[27]In 430 B.C., at the beginning of the great war between Athens and Sparta.

eign woman did long ago in examining me—for, among other things, I said to her, in nearly the same words that Agathon just used to me, that Love was a mighty god, and the beautiful his objects; and she proved to me, as I proved to him, that by my own showing, Love was neither beautiful nor good.

" 'What do you mean, Diotima?' I said. 'Is Love then ugly and evil?' 'Hush,' she cried. 'Must that be ugly which is not beautiful?' 'Certainly,' I said. 'And if something is not 202 wise, it must be ignorant? Do you not see that there is a mean between wisdom and ignorance?' 'And what may that be?' I said. 'Right opinion,' she replied, 'which, as you know, being incapable of giving a reason, is not knowledge (for how can knowledge be devoid of reason?), nor again, ignorance (for neither can ignorance attain the truth), but is clearly something that is a mean between ignorance and wisdom.' 'Quite true,' I replied. 'Do not then insist,' she said, 'that what is not beautiful is of necessity ugly, or what b is not good, evil; or infer that because, as you agree, Love is not beautiful and good, he is therefore ugly and evil; for he is a mean between them.' 'Well,' I said, 'Love is surely admitted by all to be a great god.' 'When you say by "all" do you mean by those who know or by those who do not know?' 'By *everyone*.' 'And how, Socrates,' she said with a smile, 'can Love be acknowledged to be a great god by c those who say that he is not a god at all?' 'And who are they?' I said. 'You and I are two of them,' she replied. 'How can that be?' I said. 'Elementary,' she replied; 'for you yourself would acknowledge that the gods are happy and beautiful—of course you would—or would you dare to say that any god was not?' 'Certainly not,' I replied. 'And you mean by the happy, those who are the possessors of things good or beautiful?' 'Yes.' 'And you admitted that Love, because he lacks the good and beautiful, desires them, the very things that he lacks?' 'Yes, I did.' 'But how can he be a god who has no portion in what is either good or beautiful?' 'Impossible.' 'Then you see that you also deny the divinity of Love.'

" 'What then is Love?' I asked. 'Is he mortal?' 'Of course not.' 'Well—then *what*?' 'As in the former instance, he is neither mortal nor immortal, but a mean between the two.' 'What is he, Diotima?' 'He is a great spirit [*daimon*];[28] for every spirit-like [*daimonion*] thing is intermediate between the divine and the mortal.' 'And what,' I said, 'is his power?' 'He communicates,' she replied, 'between gods and men, conveying and taking across to the gods the prayers and sacrifices of men, and to men the commands and replies of the gods; he is the mediator who fills the chasm that divides them, and therefore in him all is bound together, and through him the arts of the prophet and the priest, their sacrifices and mysteries and charms, and all prophecy and

---

[28]The Greek word *daimon* has none of the connotations of its English descendant "demon," so it has been translated as "spirit" here and throughout.

incantation find their way. For God mingles not with 203
man;[29] but through Love all the intercourse and converse
of God with man, whether awake or asleep, is carried on.
The man wise in these matters is the spiritual [*daimonios*]
man; he who is expert in other matters, such as arts or
handicrafts, is mean and vulgar. Now these spirits or intermediate powers are many and diverse, and one of them is
Love.' 'And was he born,' I said, 'of a father and a mother?'
'The tale,' she said, 'will take time; nevertheless I will tell b
you. On the day of Aphrodite's birth there was a feast of the
gods, at which the god Poros, or Efficacy, who is the son of
Metis, or Intelligence, was one of the guests. When the feast
was over, Penia, or Poverty, as is the manner on festive occasions, came about the doors to beg. Now Efficacy, who
was the worse for nectar (there was no wine in those days),
went into the garden of Zeus and fell into a heavy sleep;
and Poverty, considering her own straitened circumstances,
plotted to have a child by him, and accordingly she lay
down at his side and conceived Love, who, partly because c
he is naturally a lover of the beautiful, and because
Aphrodite is herself beautiful, and also because he was conceived on her birthday, is her follower and attendant. And

---

[29]The Greek verb for "mingles" *(meignutai)* can refer both to sexual and non-
sexual social contact, like our word "intercourse." It was Greek tradition that
after the age of the heroes, who were the products of divine unions with
mortals, the gods ceased to "mingle" directly, in any sense, with mortals.

as his parentage is, so also are his fortunes. In the first place, he is always poor, and anything but tender and fair, as the d many imagine him; and he is rough and squalid, and has no shoes, nor a house to dwell in; on the bare earth exposed he always lies under the open heaven, by the roadsides or at the doors of houses, taking his rest; and, like his mother, he is always in need. Then too, in the manner of his father, he is always scheming after what is beautiful and good; he is bold, enterprising, intense, a mighty hunter, always weaving some intrigue or other, keen in the pursuit of wisdom, fertile in resources; a lifelong philosopher,[30] awesome as an enchanter, sorcerer, sophist. He is by nature neither mortal e nor immortal, but alive and flourishing at one moment when he is in plenty, and dead at another moment, and again alive by reason of his father's nature. But that which is always flowing in is always flowing out, and so he is never in want and never in wealth; and, further, he is in a mean between ignorance and knowledge. The truth of the matter 204 is this: No god is one of wisdom's lovers[31] or desires to

---

[30]On the word "philosopher" see the next note.

[31]The words "is one of wisdom's lovers" (or "are wisdom's lovers") here and throughout are used in an effort to represent Socrates'/Diotima's idiosyncratic interpretation and use of the Greek verb *philosopheo,* which elsewhere normally means "to be a *philosophos* (philosopher),""to do what a *philosophos* does." *Philosophos,* the noun on which *philosopheo* is based, itself implies a verb-object proposition,"to love" *(philo-)* "wisdom" *(-sophos).* Socrates/Diotima emphasize the *philo-* part of *philosopheo* and thus proceed as if "to be

become wise, for he is wise already; nor is any man who is wise one of wisdom's lovers. Neither are the ignorant wisdom's lovers, nor do they desire to become wise. For herein is the evil of ignorance, that he who is neither good nor wise is nevertheless satisfied with himself: he has no desire for that of which he feels no want.' 'But who then, Diotima,' I said, 'are wisdom's lovers, if they are neither the wise nor the foolish?' 'A child may answer that question,' she ᵦ replied; 'they are those who are in a mean between the two; and Love must be one of them. For wisdom is a most beautiful thing, and Love is of the beautiful; so it necessarily follows that Love is also a philosopher, that is, one of wisdom's lovers, and being one of wisdom's lovers, he is in a mean between the wise and the ignorant. And of this too his birth is the cause; for his father is a man of means and is wise, and his mother indigent and foolish. Such, my dear Socrates, is the nature of the spirit [*daimon*] Love. The error in your conception of him was very natural, and as I imagine him ᵪ

---

a *philosophos,* i.e., wisdom lover," were the same as "to be one of Wisdom's (romantic) lovers," somewhat as if we should understand "He is a Proust lover" to mean "He is one of Proust's lovers." This move permits Socrates/Diotima to assimilate "philosophy" (and all kinds of pursuits: see Diotima's comments on moneymaking and gymnastics below in the text) to love as generally defined in their account, the yearning for that which one ipso facto does not possess—in the case of philosophers, wisdom. The paradox of this argument is like that of someone's arguing that a philharmonic (i.e., symphony orchestra) is composed of "lovers of, i.e., seekers after, harmony," thus of persons lacking and not attaining musical harmony.

from what you say, you thought that Love was the beloved, not the lover, which made you think that love was all-beautiful. For the beloved is the truly beautiful, and delicate, and perfect, and blessed; but the principle of love is of another nature, and is such as I have described.'

"I said, 'Well then, madam—since you explain so well—assuming Love to be such as you say, what is his function for mankind?' 'That, Socrates,' she replied, 'I will attempt to teach you next: his nature and birth I have already stated; and you acknowledge that Love is of the beautiful. But someone might ask us: "Why is Love of the beautiful, Socrates and Diotima?"—or, rather, let me put the question more clearly and ask: When a man loves the beautiful, what does he desire?' I answered her: 'That the beautiful may be his.' 'Still,' she said, 'the answer suggests a further question: What is given by the possession of beauty?' 'To what you have asked,' I replied, 'I have no answer ready.' 'Then,' she said, 'let me put the word "good" in the place of "the beautiful," and repeat the question once more: If he who loves, loves the good, what is it then that he loves?' 'The possession of the good,' I said. 'And what does he gain who possesses the good?' 'Happiness,' I replied; 'there is less difficulty in answering that question.' 'Yes,' she said, 'the happy are made happy by the acquisition of good things. Nor is there any need to ask why a man desires happiness; the answer is already final.' 'You are right,' I said. 'And is this wish and this desire common to all? And do all men always desire their own good, or only some men? What do you say?' 'All men,' I replied; 'the desire is common to all.' 'Then why,' she rejoined, 'are not all men, Socrates, said to love, but only some of them? Whereas you say that all men are always loving the b same things.' 'I myself wonder,' I said, 'why this is.' 'There is nothing to wonder at,' she replied; 'the reason is that one part of love is separated off and receives the name of the whole, but the other parts have other names.' 'Give an illustration,' I said. She answered me as follows: 'There is poetry, which, as you know, is complex and manifold. All creation or passage of nonbeing into being is poetry, which literally means "making," and the processes of all art are poetic, or c making, processes; and the masters of arts are all poets or makers.' 'Very true.' 'Still,' she said, 'you know that they are not called poets, but have other names; only that portion of the art which is separated off from the rest and is concerned with music and meter is termed poetry, and they who possess poetry in this sense of the word are called poets.' 'Very true,' I said. 'And the same holds of love. For you may say d generally that all desire of good and happiness is only "the great and subtle power of love";[32] but they who are drawn toward him by any other path, whether the path of money-making or gymnastics or philosophy, are not said to be in love and are not called lovers—the name of the whole is appropriated to those whose affection takes one form only; for

---

[32]This phrase appears to be a quotation.

them alone is reserved "love" and they alone are said to be
"lovers." ''It seems most likely,' I replied, 'that you are right.'
'Yes,' she added, 'and you hear people say that lovers are
ₑ seeking for their other half;[33] but I say that they are seeking
neither for the half of themselves, nor for the whole, unless
the half or the whole be also a good. And they will cut off
their own hands and feet and cast them away if they are evil;
for they love not what is their own, unless perchance there
be someone who calls what belongs to him the good, and
what belongs to another the evil. For there is nothing that
206 men love but the good. Is there anything?' 'Certainly, I
should say, that there is nothing.' 'Then,' she said, 'the simple
truth is, that men love the good.' 'Yes,' I said. 'To which must
be added that they love the possession of the good?' 'Yes, that
must be added.' 'And not only the possession, but the everlasting possession of the good?' 'That must be added too.'
'Then love,' she said, 'may be described generally as the love
of the everlasting possession of the good?' 'That is most true.'

ᵇ   " 'Then if this be the nature of love, can you tell me further,' she said, 'what is the manner of the pursuit? What are
they doing who show all this eagerness and heat which is
called love? And what is really the object that they have in
view? Answer me.' 'No, Diotima,' I replied, 'if I had known,
I should not have been so amazed at your wisdom, nor

---

[33]An unmistakable reference to Aristophanes' speech earlier, which, of
course, no real Diotima long ago could possibly have known of.

should I have come so regularly for instruction at your hands.'[34] 'Well,' she said, 'I will teach you: The object they have in view is birth in beauty, whether of body or soul.' 'I do not understand you,' I said; 'the oracle requires an explanation.' 'I will make my meaning clearer,' she replied. 'I mean to say that all humans are pregnant in their bodies and in their souls. There is a certain age at which human nature is desirous of giving birth—birth that must be in beauty and not in ugliness. The union of man and woman is this procreation, and it is a divine thing; for conception and generation are an immortal principle in the mortal creature, and in the inharmonious they can never be. But the ugly is always incompatible with the divine, and the beautiful compatible. Beauty, then, is the Goddess of Destiny and the Birth Goddess, who preside at birth,[35] and therefore, when approaching beauty, the conceiving power is propitious and delighted, and dissolves, and begets and bears fruit: at the sight of ugliness she frowns and contracts and has a sense of pain, and turns away, and shrivels up, and

---

[34]Some scholars have suspected an underlying joke here: Socrates goes to the wise Diotima "regularly for instruction" in love inasmuch as she is actually a prostitute. Plato's model for such a "learned courtesan" would have been Aspasia, Pericles' mistress, whose intellectual gifts and attainments were such that she was popularly rumored to be Pericles' (uncredited) speechwriter (cf. Plato's *Menexenus*).

[35]The goddesses Moira (Destiny) and Eileithyia (Parturition) were thought to preside over every birth.

not without a pang refrains from conception. And this is the reason why, when the hour of conception arrives, and the teeming nature is already full, there is such a flutter and e ecstasy about beauty, whose approach is the alleviation of the pain of travail. For love, Socrates, is not, as you imagine, the love of the beautiful only.' 'Of what, then?' 'The love of generation and of birth in beauty.' 'Yes,' I said. 'Yes, indeed,' she replied; 'but why of generation? Because to the mortal creature, generation is a sort of eternity and immortality, 207 and if, as has already been admitted, love is of the everlasting possession of the good, all men will necessarily desire immortality together with good: Wherefore love is of immortality.'

"All this she taught me at various times when she spoke of love. And I remember her once saying to me, 'What is the cause, Socrates, of love, and the attendant desire? Do you not see how all animals, birds, as well as beasts, in their desire for procreation, are in agony when they take the in- b fection of love, which begins with the desire for union; to which is added the care of offspring, on whose behalf the weakest are ready to battle against the strongest even to the uttermost, and to die for them, and will let themselves be tormented with hunger or suffer anything in order to maintain their young. Man may be supposed to act thus from reason; but why should animals have these passionate c feelings? Can you tell me why?' Again I replied that I did not know. She said to me, 'And do you expect ever to become a master in the art of love if you do not know this?' 'But I have told you already, Diotima, that my ignorance is the reason why I come to you; for I am conscious that I want a teacher; tell me, then, the cause of this and of the other mysteries of love.' 'If you believe' she said, 'that love is of the immortal, as we have several times acknowledged, then do not be amazed; for here again, in the case of animals, and on the same principle, too, the mortal nature is *d* seeking as far as is possible to be everlasting and immortal: and this is only to be attained by generation, because generation always leaves behind a new existence in the place of the old. For over the period in which each living thing is pronounced "alive," it is also said to be the same—for example, a man is called the same man from youth to old age, but in fact he is undergoing a perpetual process of loss and renewal—hair, flesh, bones, blood, and the whole body are *e* always changing. Which is true not only of the body, but also of the soul, whose habits, tempers, opinions, desires, pleasures, pains, fears, never remain the same in any one of us, but are always coming and going. What is still more surprising is that this is true also of the bodies of knowledge that we possess, some of which are growing and developing, others fading away, so that in respect of them we are *208* never the same; and within each body of knowledge individually the same thing happens—for there exists such a thing as "studying" only because knowledge departs from us. For "forgetting" is the departure of knowledge, while "study" preserves knowledge by introducing a renewed memory to replace the knowledge that has left, with the result that it appears to be the same. For this is the way in which all mortal things are preserved, not absolutely the same always, as the divine is, but through substitution—the old worn-out mortality leaving another new and similar existence behind. And by this mechanism, Socrates, the mortal body, or mortal anything, has its share of immortality (the immortal has it by a different mechanism). So do not then be amazed at the love that all men have of their offspring; for that universal love and interest is for the sake of immortality.'

"I was astonished at her words, and said: 'Is this really true, O thou wise Diotima?' And she answered with all the authority of an accomplished sophist: 'Of that, Socrates, you may be assured—think only of the ambition of men, and you will wonder at the senselessness of their ways, unless you consider how they are stirred by the love of an immortality of fame. They are ready to run risks greater far than they would have run for their children, and to spend money and undergo any sort of toil, and even to die, for the sake of "leaving behind them a name which shall be eternal."[36] Do you imagine that Alcestis would have died to

---

[36]A verse, from an unknown work, in the epic meter.

save Admetus, or Achilles to avenge Patroclus, or you Athenians' own Codrus[37] in order to preserve the kingdom for his sons, if they had not imagined that the memory of their virtues, which still survives among us, would be immortal? No,' she said, 'I am persuaded that all men do all things, and the better they are the more they do them, in hope of the glorious fame of immortal virtue; for they desire the immortal. Those who are pregnant in the body only betake themselves to women and beget children—this is the character of their love; their offspring, as they hope, will preserve their memory and give them the blessedness and immortality which they desire for all future time. But those who are pregnant in their souls—for there certainly exist men who generate within their souls, rather than in their bodies—conceive the kinds of things that it is proper for the soul to conceive and give birth to. And what things are these? Wisdom and virtue in general. And such creators are poets and all artists who are deserving of the name inventor. But the greatest and fairest sort of wisdom by far is that which is concerned with the ordering of states and families, and which is called temperance and justice. And he who in youth has the seed of these implanted in him and is himself inspired, when he comes to maturity desires to

e

209

b

---

[37]Mythical king of Athens who, when it was foretold to an enemy that Athens could not be conquered if Codrus were killed, disguised himself and allowed himself to be killed, and thus saved the Athenians from subjugation.

beget and generate. He wanders about seeking beauty in which to beget offspring—for in ugliness he will beget nothing—and because he is in pain of travail he embraces the beautiful rather than the ugly body; above all when he finds a beautiful and noble and talented soul, he embraces the two in one person, and to such a one he is full of speech

c about virtue and the nature and pursuits of a good man; and he tries to educate him; and by touching the beautiful and consorting with him he gives birth to and propagates that which he had conceived long before, both when with him and through recollecting him when apart, and together with him he tends that which was brought forth; and they are married by a far nearer tie and have a closer friendship than those who beget mortal children, for the children who are their common offspring are fairer and

d more immortal. Who, when he thinks of Homer and Hesiod and other great poets, would not rather have their children than ordinary human ones? Who would not emulate them in the creation of children such as theirs, which have preserved their memory and given them everlasting glory? Or who would not have such children as Lycurgus[38] left behind him to be the saviors not only of Lacedaemon but of Hellas, as one may say? There is Solon, too, who is the revered father of Athenian laws; and many others there are

e in many other places, both among Hellenes and barbarians,

---

[38]The legendary framer of the Spartan constitution.

who have given to the world many noble works, and have been the parents of virtue of every kind; and many temples have been raised in their honor for the sake of children such as theirs; whereas none were ever raised in honor of anyone for the sake of his mortal children.

" 'These are the lesser mysteries of love,' she said, 'into which you also, Socrates, may be initiated; to the greater and more hidden ones which are the crown of these, and 210 to which, if you pursue them in a right spirit, they will lead, I know not whether you will be able to attain. But I will do my utmost to inform you, and do you follow if you can.[39] For he who would proceed aright in this matter should begin in youth to visit beautiful bodies; and first, if he be guided by his instructor aright, to love one such body only, and in it he should engender beautiful thoughts; and soon he will of himself perceive that the beauty of one body is akin to the beauty of another; and then, if beauty b of appearance is his pursuit, how foolish would he be not to recognize that the beauty present in all bodily forms is one and the same! And when he perceives this he will abate his violent love of the one, which he will despise and deem a small thing, and will become a lover of all beautiful bodily forms; in the next stage he will consider that the beauty

---

[39]From this point through to the end of her speech Diotima's language draws heavily on that of the Eleusinian mysteries, celebrated annually in Attica.

of the soul is more honorable than the beauty of the body, so that someone even of slight beauty, but virtuous in soul

c satisfies him, and he loves and cares for him, and brings to birth arguments of the kind to improve the young, until he is compelled to contemplate and see the beauty of institutions and laws, and to understand that the beauty of them all is of one family, and that personal beauty is a trifle; and after laws and institutions he will go on to the sciences, that

d he may see their beauty, being not servilely in love with the beauty of one youth or man or institution, himself a slave, mean and small-minded, but drawing toward and contemplating the vast sea of beauty, he will create many fair and noble thoughts and notions in boundless love of wisdom; until on that shore he grows and waxes strong, and at last the vision is revealed to him of a single science, which is the

e science of beauty everywhere. To this I will proceed; please give me your very best attention.

" 'He who has been instructed thus far in the things of love, and who has learned to see the beautiful in due order and succession, when he comes toward the end will suddenly have a vision of wondrous beauty (and this, Socrates, is the final cause of all our former toils)—a beauty that in

211 the first place is everlasting, not growing and decaying, or waxing and waning; secondly, not beautiful in one point of view and ugly in another, or at one time or in one relation or at one place beautiful, at another time or in another relation or at another place ugly, as if beautiful to some and

ugly to others, nor will beauty appear to him in the likeness of a face or hands or any other part of the bodily
frame, or in any form of expression or knowledge, or exist-
ing in any other being, as for example, in an animal, or in
heaven, or in earth, or in any other place; but beauty will b
be revealed to him to be absolute, separate, simple, and
everlasting, which, without diminution and without in-
crease, or any change, is imparted to the ever-growing and
perishing beauties of all other things. He who, ascending
from these by means of proper and correct pederastic love,
begins to perceive *that* beauty is not far from the end. And
the correct order of going, or being led by another, to the c
things of love is to begin from the beauties of earth and
mount ever upward for the sake of that other beauty, using
these as steps only, and from one going on to two, and from
two to all beautiful bodies, and from beautiful bodies to
beautiful practices, and from beautiful practices to beautiful notions, until from beautiful notions he arrives at the
notion of absolute beauty, and at last knows what the
essence of beauty is. This, my dear Socrates,' said the d
stranger from Mantineia, 'is that life above all others which
man should live, in the contemplation of beauty absolute; a
beauty that, if you once beheld it, you would see not to be
like that of gold, and garments, and beautiful boys and
youths, whose presence now entrances you; and you and
many a one would be content to live seeing them only and
conversing with them, without food or drink, if that were

possible—you only want to look at them and to be with them. But what if man had eyes to see the true beauty— the divine beauty, I mean, pure and clear and unalloyed, not clogged with the pollutions of human flesh and complexion and all the other vanities of mortal life—do you think it an ignoble life for a person to be gazing *there* and contemplating *that* with the suitable instrument, the mind's eye, and consorting with *that*? Do you not perceive that *there* alone will it happen to him, when he sees the beautiful with that instrument with which it must be seen, to give birth not to images of virtue, since he is not laying hold of an image, but to her true progeny, since he has hold of true virtue? And is it not possible for him, by giving birth to and nourishing true virtue, to become the beloved of God, and to become, if any of humankind does, immortal?'

"Such, Phaedrus—and I speak not only to you, but to all of you—were the words of Diotima; and I am persuaded of their truth. And being persuaded of them, I try to persuade others that in the attainment of this end, human nature will not easily find a helper better than Love. And therefore, also, I say that every man ought to honor him as I myself honor him, and I myself honor his works and cultivate them intensively, and exhort others to do the same, and praise the power and manliness of Love, according to the measure of my ability, now and forever.

"The words which I have spoken, you, Phaedrus, may call an encomium of Love, or anything else you please."

When Socrates had done speaking, the company applauded, and Aristophanes was beginning to say something in answer to the allusion that Socrates had made to his own speech, when suddenly there was a great knocking at the door of the house, as of revelers, and the voice of a flute-girl was heard. Agathon told the slaves to go and see who were the intruders. "If they are friends of ours," he said, "invite them in, but if not, say that the drinking is over." A little while afterward they heard the voice of Alcibiades in the court, intensely drunk, bellowing and demanding, "Where is Agathon? Lead me to Agathon." And at length, supported by the flute-girl and some of his attendants, he found his way to them. "Gentlemen! Hello!" he said, appearing at the door crowned with a massive garland of ivy and violets, his head flowing with ribbons. "Will you have a very drunken man as a companion of your revels? Or shall I crown Agathon, which was my intention in coming, and go away? For I was unable to come yesterday, and therefore I am here today, carrying on my head these ribbons, that taking them from my own head, I may crown the head of this most beautiful and most accomplished of men. Will you laugh at me because I am drunk? Yet I know very well that I am speaking the truth, although you may laugh. But first tell me, if I come in, shall we have the understanding of which I spoke? Will you drink with me or not?"

The company were vociferous in begging that he would take his place among them, and Agathon specially invited him. Thereupon he was led in by the people who were with him; and as he was being led, intending to crown Agathon, he took the ribbons from his own head and held them in front of his eyes; he was thus prevented from seeing Socrates, who made way for him when he saw him, and

b Alcibiades took the vacant place between Agathon and Socrates, and in taking the place he embraced Agathon and crowned him. "Take off his sandals," said Agathon, "and let him make a third on the same couch."

"By all means; but who makes the third partner in our revels?" said Alcibiades, turning round and starting up as he caught sight of Socrates. "By Heracles," he said, "what is this? Is Socrates here? You lay here, once again ambushing

c me, as your way is, leaping out where I least expected you would be. And now what have you to say for yourself: why are you lying *here,* where I perceive that you have contrived to find a place not by a joker or lover of jokes, like Aristophanes, but by the most beautiful of the company?"

Socrates turned to Agathon and said, "I must ask you to protect me, Agathon; for my love affair with this man has become quite a troublesome problem. Since I became his

d lover, I have never been allowed to speak to any other beauty, or so much as to look at them. If I do, he goes wild with envy and jealousy, and not only abuses me but can hardly keep his hands off me, and at this moment he may do me some harm. Please see to this, and either reconcile me to him, or, if he attempts violence, protect me, as I am in bodily fear of his mad and passionate attempts."

"There can never be reconciliation between you and me," said Alcibiades; "but for the present I will defer your chastisement. And I must beg you, Agathon, to give me back some of the ribbons that I may crown this extraordinary head of his—I would not have him complain of me for crowning you, and neglecting him, who in conversation is the conqueror of all mankind; and this not only once, as you were the day before yesterday, but always." Whereupon, taking some of the ribbons, he crowned Socrates, and again reclined.

Then he said, "You seem, my friends, to be sober, which is a thing not to be endured; you must drink—for that was the agreement under which I was admitted—and I choose as master of the feast, until you are well drunk, myself. Let us have a large goblet, Agathon, or rather," he said, addressing the slave, "bring me that wine cooler." The wine cooler that had caught his eye was a vessel holding more than two quarts—this he filled and emptied, and bade the slave fill it again for Socrates. "Observe, my friends," said Alcibiades, "that this ingenious trick of mine will have no effect on Socrates, for he can drink any quantity of wine and not be at all nearer being drunk." Socrates took a drink after the slave poured for him.

Eryximachus said, "What is this, Alcibiades? Are we to

b have neither conversation nor singing over our cups, but simply to drink as if we were parched?"

Alcibiades replied, "Hail, worthy son of a most wise and worthy sire!"

"The same to you," said Eryximachus; "but what shall we do?"

"That I leave to you," said Alcibiades. " 'For a doctor's life is worth many others'.[40] Therefore prescribe and we will obey. What do you want?"

"Well," said Eryximachus, "before you appeared we had passed a resolution that each one of us in turn should make c a speech in praise of Love, and as good a one as he could. The turn was passed round from left to right; and as all of us have spoken, and you have not spoken but have well drunken, you ought to speak, and then impose upon Socrates any task you please, and he on his right-hand neighbor, and so on."

"That is good, Eryximachus," said Alcibiades, "and yet the comparison of a drunken man's speech with those of sober men is hardly fair; and I should like to know, O holy one, whether you really believe what Socrates was just now d saying; for I can assure you that the very reverse is the fact, and that if I praise anyone but himself in his presence, whether God or man, he will hardly keep his hands off me."

---

[40] *Iliad* 11. 514.

"Hush," said Socrates.

"No, by god, don't contradict me," said Alcibiades, "for with *you* here I couldn't praise *anyone* else."

"Well, then," said Eryximachus, "if you like, praise Socrates."

"What do you think, Eryximachus?" said Alcibiades. "Shall I attack him and inflict the punishment before you all?"

"Hey! Just what do you have in mind?" said Socrates. "Are you going to make fun of me? Is that the meaning of your praise?"

"I am going to speak the truth, if you will permit me."

"I not only permit, but I command you to speak the truth."

"Then I will begin at once," said Alcibiades, "and if I say anything that is not true, you may interrupt me, if you will, and say, 'That is a lie,' though my intention is to speak the truth. But you must not wonder if I speak every which way as things come into my mind; for the fluent and orderly enumeration of all your singularities is not an easy task for a man in my condition.

"And now, gentlemen, I shall praise Socrates in a figure that will appear to him to be a caricature, and yet I speak not to make fun of him but only for the truth's sake. I say that he is exactly like the busts of Silenus, which are set up in the statuaries' shops, holding pipes and flutes in their mouths; and when they are made to open in two, they are

revealed to have images of gods inside them. I say also that
he is like Marsyas the satyr. You yourself will not deny,
Socrates, that your face is like that of a satyr. Yes, and there
is a resemblance in other points too. For example, you are
a bully, as I can prove by witnesses, if you will not confess.
And are you not a flute player? That you are, and a per-
former far more wonderful than Marsyas. He indeed with
c instruments used to charm the souls of men by the power
of his breath, and the players of his music do so still: for the
melodies of Olympus are derived from Marsyas, who
taught them to Olympus, and these, whether they are
played by a great master or by a miserable flute-girl, have a
power that no others have; they alone possess the soul and
reveal those who have need of gods and mysteries, because
their music is divine. But you produce the same effect with
your words only, and do not require the flute: that is the
d only difference between you and him. When we hear any
other speaker, even a very good one, he produces absolutely
no effect upon us, or not much, whereas the mere fragments of your words, even at second hand, and however
imperfectly repeated, amaze and possess the souls of every
man, woman, and child who comes within hearing of
them. And if I were not afraid that you would think me
hopelessly drunk, I would have testified under oath to the
influence that they have always had and still have over me.
e For my heart leaps within me, more than that of any Cory-
bantian reveler, and my eyes rain tears when I hear this

man's talk. And I observe that many others are affected in the same manner. I have heard Pericles and other great orators, and I thought that they spoke well, but I never had any similar feeling; my soul was not thrown into a tumult by them, nor was it angry at the thought of my own slavish state. But this Marsyas has often brought me to such a pass that I have felt as if I could hardly endure the life that 216 I am leading (this, Socrates, you will admit); and I am still now conscious that if I should lend my ears to him, I would not withstand him but would suffer the same thing again. For he makes me confess that I ought not to live as I do, neglecting the wants of my own soul, and busying myself with the concerns of the Athenians; therefore I hold my ears and tear my unwilling self away from him, that I not grow old sitting here at his feet. And he is the only person who ever made me ashamed, which you might think not b to be in my nature; there is no one else before whom I feel shame. For I know that I cannot answer him or say that I ought not to do as he bids, but when I leave his presence, the love of advancement gets the better of me. And therefore I run away from him like a fugitive, and when I see him, I am ashamed of what I have confessed to him. Many a time have I wished that he were dead, and yet I know that c I should be much more sorry than glad if he were to die: so that I am at my wit's end.

"And this is what I and many others have suffered from the flute-playing of this satyr. Yet hear me once more while

I show you how exact the image is, and how marvelous his power. For let me tell you, none of you know him, but I will reveal him to you; having begun, I must go on. You have all observed that he is sexually attracted to the beautiful. He is always with them and is always being smitten by them, and then again he knows nothing and is ignorant of all things—such is the appearance he puts on. Is he not like a Silenus in this? To be sure, he is: his outer mask is the carved head of the Silenus; but, O my companions in drink, when he is opened, what temperance there is residing within! I can assure you that it doesn't matter a whit to him if a person is beautiful—he is contemptuous of the whole thing to a degree not one of you could imagine; likewise with wealth and any other attribute worshiped by the masses. He regards all these possessions as worthless, and, I tell you, he regards *us* as worthless: all his life is spent mocking and flouting at mankind. But there is seriousness in him. I don't know if any of you have seen him opened up, and the sacred relics that lie within; but I saw once, and they seemed so golden and of such fascinating beauty that I concluded that whatever Socrates commanded must be done.

"Now, I fancied that he was seriously enamored of my youthful beauty, and I thought that I should therefore have a grand opportunity of hearing him tell what he knew, for I had a wonderful opinion of the attractions of my youth. In the prosecution of this design, when I next went to him,

I sent away the attendant who usually accompanied me (I b will confess the whole truth, and beg you to listen; and if I speak falsely, then you, Socrates, expose the falsehood). Well, he and I were alone together, and I thought that when there was nobody with us, I should hear him speak the language that lovers use to their loves when they are by themselves, and I was delighted. Nothing of the sort; he conversed as usual, and spent the day with me and then went away. Afterwards I challenged him to the palaestra; c and he wrestled and closed with me several times when there was no one present; I fancied that I might succeed in this manner. Not a bit; I made no headway with him. Lastly, as I had failed hitherto, I thought that I must make a direct assault and, as I had begun, not give him up, but see how matters stood between him and me. So I invited him to sup with me, just as if he were a comely youth and I a design-ing lover. He was not easily persuaded to come; he did, however, after a while accept the invitation, and when he came the first time, he wanted to go away at once as soon as supper was over, and I had not the face to detain him. d The second time, still in pursuance of my design, after we had supped, I went on conversing far into the night, and when he wanted to go away, I pretended that the hour was late and insisted that he remain. So he lay down on the couch next to mine, the same on which he had supped, and there was no one but ourselves sleeping in the apartment. All this may be told without shame to anyone. But what e follows I could hardly tell you if I were sober. Yet as the proverb says, 'In vino veritas,' both with boys and without them;[41] and therefore I must speak. Nor, again, should I be justified in concealing the lofty actions of Socrates when I come to praise him. Moreover I have felt the serpent's sting; and he who has suffered, as they say, is willing to relate his sufferings to his fellow sufferers only, as they alone will be likely to understand him, and will not be extreme in judging of the sayings or doings that have been wrung from his agony. For I have been bitten by more than a viper's tooth; I have known in my soul, or in my heart, or in some other part, that worst of pangs, more violent in a not-untalented youth than any serpent's tooth, the pang of philosophy, which will make a man say or do anything. And you whom I see around me, you Phaedruses and Agathons and Eryximachuses and Pausaniases and Aristodemuses and Aristophaneses,[42] all of you, and I need not say Socrates himself, have had experience of the same madness and passion in your longing after wisdom. Therefore listen and excuse my doings then and my sayings now. But let the house slaves

---

[41]The exact meaning of the proverb quoted, or adapted, by Alcibiades—especially the words "both with boys and without them" (which can also mean "with slaves and without them")—is not known.

[42]The plurals suggest "Phaedrus and people like him," etc., but also raise the possibility that Alcibiades is seeing double.

and other profane and unmannered persons close up the doors of their ears.

"When the lamp was put out and the slaves had gone away, I thought that I must be plain with him and have no more ambiguity. So I gave him a shake, and I said, 'Socrates, are you asleep?' 'No,' he said. 'Do you know what I am meditating?' 'What are you meditating?' he said. 'I think,' I replied, 'that of all the lovers I have ever had, you are the only one who is worthy of me, and you appear to be too modest to raise the subject with me. Now, this is how matters stand with me: I feel that I should be a fool to refuse you this or any other favor, and therefore I come to lay at your feet all that I have and all that my friends have, in the hope that you will assist me in the way of virtue, which I prize above all things, and in which I believe that you can help me better than anyone else. And I should certainly have more reason to be ashamed of what wise men would say if I were to refuse to gratify a man such as you, than of what the world, who are mostly fools, would say of me if I did.' To these words he replied in the ironical manner which is so characteristic of him: 'Alcibiades, my friend, you are, as it seems, a very shrewd bargainer, if what you say is true, and if there really is in me any power by which you may become better; obviously you must see in me some rare beauty of a kind infinitely higher than any that I see in you. And therefore, if you mean to share with me and to exchange beauty for beauty, you will have greatly the advantage of me; you will gain true beauty in return for the appearance of beauty—like Diomedes, "gold in exchange for bronze."[43] But look again, blessed friend, and see whether you have failed to notice that I am in fact nothing at all. The mind's eye begins to grow critical when the bodily eye fails, and it will be a long time before you get old.' Hearing this, I said, 'I have told you my purpose, which is quite serious, and so please consider what you think best for you and me.' 'That is good,' he said; 'at some other time then we will consider and act as seems best about this and about other matters.' At which words I fancied that he was smitten, and that the words I had uttered like arrows had wounded him, and so, without waiting to hear more, I got up and, throwing my coat about him, crept under his threadbare cloak, as the time of year was winter, and there I lay during the night, having this wonderful monster in my arms. This again, Socrates, will not be denied by you. And yet, notwithstanding all, he was so superior to my solicitations, so contemptuous and derisive and disdainful of my beauty—which really, as I fancied, had some attractions—

219

b

c

---

[43]In *Iliad* 6. 232–236 the Trojan ally Glaucus offers as a gesture of guest-friendship to exchange armor with the Greek Diomedes: Glaucus' armor was made of gold, Diomedes' of bronze, and Homer comments after the exchange is made that Zeus had removed Glaucus' wits. "Gold for bronze" (or "Bronze for gold") became and remains proverbial.

hear, O judges, for judges you shall be of the haughty virtue of Socrates: in the morning (let all the gods and goddesses be my witnesses) I got up, together with Socrates, having passed the night no differently than if I had shared a bed d with a father or an elder brother.

"What do you suppose must have been my feelings, after this rejection, at the thought of my own dishonor? And yet I could not help wondering at his natural temperance and self-restraint and manliness. I never imagined that I could have met with a man such as he is in wisdom and endurance. And therefore I could not be angry with him or renounce his company, any more than I could hope to win him. For I well know that if Ajax could not be wounded by e steel, much less could he by money; and my only chance of captivating him by my personal attractions had failed. So I was at my wit's end; no one was ever more hopelessly enslaved by another. All this happened before he and I went on the expedition to Potidaea; there we messed together, and I had the opportunity of observing his extraordinary power of sustaining hardship. His endurance was simply incredible when, being cut off from our supplies, we were compelled to go without food—on such occasions, which often happen in time of war, he was superior not only to me but to everybody; there was no one to be compared with him. Yet at feasts, in times of abundance, he was the 220 only person who had any real powers of enjoyment; in particular, though not willing to drink, he could, if compelled,

beat us all at that; and what is most astounding of all, no human being has ever seen Socrates drunk—and his powers, if I am not mistaken, will be tested tonight before long. His fortitude in enduring cold was also extraordinary.
b There was a severe frost, for the winter in that region is really tremendous, and everybody else either remained indoors or, if they went out, had on an amazing quantity of clothes, and were well shod, and had their feet swathed in felt and fleeces: in the midst of this, Socrates, with his bare feet on the ice and in his ordinary dress, marched better than the other soldiers, who had shoes, and they looked daggers at him because he seemed to despise them.

"I have told you one tale, and now I must tell you another, which is worth hearing, 'of the doings and sufferings
c of this mighty man,'[44] while he was on the expedition. One morning he was thinking about something that he could not resolve; he would not give it up, but continued thinking from early dawn until noon—there he stood fixed in thought; and at noon attention was drawn to him, and the rumor ran through the wondering crowd that Socrates had been standing and thinking about something ever since the break of day. At last, in the evening after supper, some Ionians, out of curiosity (I should explain that this was not in winter but in summer), brought out their mats and slept in the open air that they might watch him and see whether he

---

[44]*Odyssey* 4. 242, spoken in reference to Odysseus.

would stand all night. There he stood until the following morning; and with the return of light he offered up a prayer to the sun, and went his way. I will also tell, if you please— and indeed I am bound to tell—of his courage in battle; for who but he saved my life? Now this was the engagement in which I received the prize of valor: for I was wounded e and he would not leave me, but he rescued me and my weapons; and he ought to have received the prize of valor, which the generals wanted to confer on me partly on account of my rank, and I told them so (this, again, Socrates will not impeach or deny), but he was more eager than the generals that I and not he should have the prize. There was another occasion on which his behavior was very remarkable—in the flight of the army after the battle of Delium, 221 where he served among the heavy-armed infantry. He and Laches[45] were retreating, for the troops were in flight, and I met them and told them not to be discouraged, and promised to remain with them. On this occasion I had a better opportunity of seeing him than at Potidaea (for I was myself on horseback, and therefore comparatively out of danger), especially of seeing how much he surpassed Laches in presence of mind. He seemed to me there, Aristophanes, b just as he is in the streets of Athens, as you describe,[46] 'stalk-

---

[45]An Athenian with a distinguished military career.
[46]Alcibiades adapts line 362 of Aristophanes' viciously hostile comedy about Socrates, *The Clouds*.

ing like a pelican, and looking from side to side,' calmly contemplating enemies as well as friends, and making very intelligible to anybody, even from a distance, that whoever attacked *this* man would be guaranteed to meet with a stout resistance; and in this way he and his companion escaped— for as a rule this is the sort of man who is never touched in war; only those are pursued who are running away head-

c long.

"Many are the marvels that I might narrate in praise of Socrates; most of his ways might perhaps be paralleled in another man, but his absolute unlikeness to any human being that is or ever has been is perfectly astonishing. You may imagine Brasidas[47] and others to have been like Achilles; or you may imagine Nestor and Antenor[48] to have been like Pericles; and the same may be said of other fa-

d mous men, but of this strange being and his talk you will never be able to find any likeness, however remote, either among men who now are or who ever have been—other than that which I have already suggested of Silenus and the satyrs; and they represent in a figure not only himself, but his words. For although I forgot to mention this to you be-

e fore, his words are like the images of Silenus that open; they are ridiculous when you first hear them; he clothes himself

---

[47]Spartan general who died in 422 B.C..

[48]The legendary wise councilors of the Greeks and Trojans, respectively, during the Trojan War.

in language that is like the skin of the wanton satyr—for his talk is of pack asses and smiths and cobblers and curriers, and he is always repeating the same things in the same words, so that any ignorant or inexperienced person might feel disposed to laugh at him; but he who opens the bust 222 and sees what is within will find that they are the only words that have a meaning in them, and also the most divine, abounding in beautiful images of virtue, and of the widest comprehension, or rather extending to the whole duty of him who would be a good and honorable man.

"This, friends, is my praise of Socrates. I have added my blame of him and told you of his ill-treatment of me; and he has ill-treated not only me, but Charmides the son of b Glaucon, and Euthydemus the son of Diocles, and many others in the same way—beginning as their lover, he has ended by reversing roles and making *them* pay their addresses to *him*. Wherefore I say to you, Agathon, 'Be not deceived by him; learn from me and take warning, and do not be "a fool and learn by experience," as the proverb says.' "[49]

When Alcibiades had finished, there was a laugh at his c outspokenness; for he seemed to be still in love with Socrates. "You are sober, Alcibiades," said Socrates, "or you would never have gone to such lengths to hide the purpose of your praises, for all this long story is only an ingenious

---

[49]The proverb alluded to occurs at *Iliad* 17.32 (among other places): "When something is over and done even a fool recognizes it."

circumlocution, of which the point comes in almost as an afterthought at the end, as if you hadn't spoken the whole speech with this aim in mind: to cause a quarrel between me and Agathon. Your notion is that I ought to love you and nobody else, and that you and you only ought to love Agathon. But the plot of this Satyric or Silenic drama has been detected, and you must not allow him, Agathon, to set us at variance."

d

"I believe you are right," said Agathon, "and I am disposed to think that his intention in placing himself between you and me was only to divide us; but he shall gain nothing by that move; for I will go and lie on the couch next to you."

e

"Yes, yes," replied Socrates, "by all means come here and lie on the couch below me."

"Oh no!" said Alcibiades. "Once again I am abused by this man; he is determined to get the better of me at every turn. I beseech you, at least allow Agathon to lie between us."

"Certainly not," said Socrates; "as you praised me, and I in turn ought to praise my neighbor on the right, he will be out of order and praise me again, won't he, when he ought rather to be praised by me. So I must entreat you to consent to this, and not be jealous, for I have a great desire to praise the youth."

223

"Hurrah!" cried Agathon. "There is no possibility that I

will stay here, Alcibiades, but I will change places immediately, in order to be praised by Socrates."

"This is *just* what I was talking about—the usual way," said Alcibiades; "where Socrates is, no one else has any chance with the pretty; and now how readily has he invented a specious reason for attracting Agathon to himself."

Agathon arose in order that he might take his place on b the couch by Socrates, when suddenly a band of revelers entered and spoiled the order of the banquet. Someone who was going out having left the door open, they had found their way in and made themselves at home; great confusion ensued, and every one was compelled to drink large quantities of wine. Aristodemus said that Eryximachus, Phaedrus, and others went away—he himself fell asleep and, as the nights were long, took a good rest: he was c awakened toward daybreak by a crowing of cocks, and when he awoke, the others were either asleep or had gone away; there remained only Socrates, Aristophanes, and Agathon, who were drinking out of a large goblet, which they passed round, and Socrates was discoursing to them. Aristodemus was only half awake, and he did not hear the beginning of the discourse; the chief thing that he remem- d bered was Socrates compelling the other two to acknowledge that the genius of comedy was the same as that of tragedy, and that the true artist in tragedy was an artist in comedy also. To this they were constrained to assent, being drowsy, and not quite following the argument. And first of all Aristophanes dropped off, then, when the day was already dawning, Agathon. Socrates, having seen them to sleep, rose to depart, Aristodemus, as his manner was, following him. At the Lyceum he took a bath, and passed the day as usual. In the evening he retired to rest at his own home.

A NOTE ON THE TYPE

The principal text of this Modern Library edition
was set in a digitized version of Bembo, a typeface
based on an old-style Roman face that was used
for Cardinal Bembo's tract *De Aetna* in 1495.
Bembo was cut by Francisco Griffo in the early
sixteenth century. The Lanston Monotype
Machine Company of Philadelphia brought
the well-proportioned letter forms of
Bembo to the United States
in the 1930s.